THREE MEN
SIX LIVES

Other Works by
BERNIE S. SIEGEL, MD

Love, Medicine and Miracles (published 1986)
How to Live Between Office Visits (published 1993)
Peace, Love and Healing (published 1998)
Prescriptions for Living (published 1999)
365 Prescriptions for the Soul (published 2003)
Help Me to Heal (published 2003)
Smudge Bunny (published 2004)
101 Exercises for the Soul (published 2005)
Love, Magic and Mudpies (published 2006)
Buddy's Candle (published 2008)
Faith, Hope and Healing (published 2009)
The Art of Healing (published 2013)
A Book of Miracles (published 2014)
Love, Animals and Miracles (published 2015)
Words and Swords poetry books
No Endings, Only Beginnings (published 2020)
When You Realize How Perfect Everything Is (published 2020)

THREE MEN
SIX LIVES

BERNIE S. SIEGEL, MD

Sacred Stories

PUBLISHING

Three Men, Six Lives

Bernie S. Siegel, MD

Tradepaper ISBN: 978-1-945026-72-0

Electronic ISBN: 978-1-945026-73-7

Library of Congress Control Number: 2020943129

Published by Sacred Stories Publishing, Fort Lauderdale, FL

Printed in the United States of America

AUTHOR NOTE

Dear Everybody,

As a four-year-old, while home in bed with an ear infection, I unscrewed the dial on my toy telephone, being curious about its workings. Having seen the carpenters working in our home put nails in their mouth; I put the toy phone pieces in my mouth and accidentally aspirated them. Whenever I write or speak about it, I relive my distressingly painful struggle to breathe, followed by my feeling of total serenity as I left my body.

At the time, if given the choice, I would have gladly chosen death over life. It didn't seem strange to me that "I" could see the boy on the bed choking to death, because for me seeing was a normal experience. If I had been born blind, I would have had some very interesting questions to ask about how I could still see and think.

I realize now we are not our bodies and that I wasn't dying: my body was. I knew the boy on the bed was not me. My consciousness continued to function in every way.

Now back to the present. A few years ago, while conversing over the phone about how busy I was, my friend responded, "Why are you living this life?" The question spontaneously induced visions of a past life as a knight. I believe this happened in Ireland because of certain events in my life, including a child in an Irish family being named after me after I participated in his safe birth. His name is Brady because Bernie wasn't Irish enough. I am sure I became a surgeon and rescued animals as a reaction to my killing with a sword, while now, as a surgeon, I am healing people with one.

The personal experiences I am sharing with you through *Three Men, Six Lives* have convinced me we are more than physical bodies. One of the stories is my story, while the characters are my creations, so that the privacy of those involved is maintained.

It is time we open our minds, start asking questions about consciousness and the nature of life, and accept the answers provided by our experiences. Life is an unexplained miracle. I believe understanding our inner space is far more important for the survival of our species than exploring outer space. I also believe extraterrestrials/aliens, when and if we encounter them, won't be essentially different from us. Despite their varied backgrounds, Einstein and Jung, had much in common, and a meaningful relationship. We still have much to learn about life and creation.

I consider this book to be what I call a nonfiction novel. Nonfiction in the sense that it shares the true experiences of people I know, and fiction because I created the characters. I dedicate this book to all the lives we've lived, and to the soul mates who accompany us, as we consciously attend the school of life.

I know every character in this book is a part of me, my wife, and our life. I cry when I read the closing chapters and statements of the characters because they are speaking my truth also.

May *Three Men, Six Lives* inspire you to achieve the benefits of a whole life policy and enable you to become a true-life assurance agent for others.

Peace,
Bernie S. Siegel, MD

To know that we maintain an identity independent of the physical body is proof enough of immortality.
-Ernest Holmes

The final belief is to believe in a fiction, which you know to be a fiction, there being nothing else. The exquisite truth is to know that it is a fiction and that you believe in it willingly.
-Wallace Stevens

It is in this sense that case histories are fundamental to depth psychology. They move us from the fiction of reality to the reality of fiction.
-James Hillman

'Tis not that Dying hurts us so —
'Tis living — hurts us more —
But Dying — is a different way —
A Kind behind the Door —
-Emily Dickinson

In the time of your life, live—so that in that good time there shall be no ugliness or death for yourself or for any life your life touches. In the time of your life, live—so that in that wondrous time you shall not add to the misery and sorrow of the world, but shall smile to the infinite delight and mystery of it.
-William Saroyan

There is only one thing that speaks the truth, a story. Fiction, Poetry, Lyrics and every written word shares the truth because the authors are telling a story about their experience.
There was consciousness and consciousness was with God and consciousness was God.
-Bernie S. Siegel, MD

CHAPTER 1

Salvatore Petonito's life revolved around routines. Every morning he began the day reading the *Topeka Sentinel* while having breakfast at the Athenian Diner. Sal didn't need to order breakfast because his ritual included the same specific meal each day, so the staff was always prepared for his arrival the same time every morning. The first Friday of every month Sal would tear off the page containing the local animal shelter's photographs of pets available for adoption, fold it carefully, and place it in his jacket pocket. When he arrived home from work that evening Sal would swing over to the kitchen table on his crutches, where he would unfold it, and place it for his wife Rosa to see. Sal always relied on her well-rehearsed response:

"Sweetheart, I will not have a barking dog in our house and little pieces of fur all over the furniture."

Though he remained ever hopeful, Sal truly believed that if his lifelong dream was to ever become a reality, it would require divine intervention.

Today's entire animal shelter page was devoted to the story of terrier, who had been struck by a car and severely injured. Interviews with the people who rescued the dog, the shelter's staff, and the veterinarian filled the page:

I didn't expect him to survive due to his internal injuries, but his will to live was amazing. That's why the staff named him Survivor. The majority of people in town either prayed for him or donated money to cover his medical expenses, but his deformity has diminished their interest in adopting him. The thought of euthanizing him is heartbreaking, but the shelter is filled to capacity and he's been here well beyond the legal time limit. If he isn't adopted this week, his story will have a tragic ending.

Mid-bite, Sal set down his fork and folded the page. After tucking it into his shirt pocket, he placed his waitress's tip on the table and exited the diner. Spiro, the diner's owner, shrugged at his silent, unexpected departure.

Sal drove straight to the animal shelter. Upon entering the waiting room, Sal held up the newspaper page.

"I'd like to see this dog."

Survivor was brought to the visitor's area and walked directly over to where Sal was sitting, as if he knew him and was following his commands. Though they both remained silent, it was obvious their wounded souls were communicating. After several minutes, Sal spun around, grabbed his crutches, and started swinging them across the room. The staff assumed Sal was leaving and started to take Survivor back to his kennel, but the dog evaded their grasp by slipping into the space beneath Sal's stump, moving in rhythm with Sal's crutches as he swung over to the front desk.

"For the record, his new name is Tripod," Sal said.

After filling out the papers and paying the adoption fee, Sal and Tripod exited the animal shelter their strides in perfect sync, as if they had spent a lifetime together.

"Young fella, we're family and going to be spending a lot of time together. So, let's get to know each other."

The two headed over to the town green where Sal seated himself while patting the bench. "Jumpee upee." With a little help, Tripod jumped onto the bench beside Sal then placed his head in Sal's lap.

"Let me tell you where I'm coming from. The only time I have ever left this town was out of a sense of duty, which overcame my hatred of war, but not my horror at having to participate in it. A drunk driver did your damage. A world war and a landmine did mine." Sal patted his stump. "Nations, races, and religions fight wars, but people suffer and die. Lives were meant to be love stories. Someday maybe we'll wake up to the fact that we're all members of the same family, with the same Father, the same color inside, and the same at both ends of the rifle. You're more likely to die in the arms of a loved one than I am. Hey, you listening?"

Tripod placed his lone front paw on Sal's chest and began licking his chin. It was a moment Sal had waited a lifetime for, something his parents and wife could never understand. He knew he would never feel abandoned again.

He hugged Tripod to his chest. "I'm not going to hide the truth and let them amputate my spirit. There's no prosthesis for that. We'll never be perfect, but we can still be complete. Who knows? Maybe what we shed enhances our other features, and it sure doesn't stop us from being able to love and be loved."

Sal stroked the dog's thick, white matted fur. "Somebody didn't love you."

"My psychiatrist couldn't understand. He had eyes and ears to see and hear with, but no heart to understand with. Said I had post-traumatic stress disorder and sent me home on medication instead of honoring my attitude and potential. He was treating the result but not the cause of my troubles. He medicated a diagnosis but didn't treat me and my story."

Tripod glanced up at Sal as if he truly understood.

"Drugs don't change anything. They just make you numb. Nobody understood. If I'd been a dog, my wife probably would have put me out of my misery. When Rosa's brother came home on leave, he came over to visit. I can still hear Rosa." Sal grew quiet as he recalled the time of his discharge...

"If they don't readmit him, I don't know what I'm going to do. I can't live like this. I know it sounds terrible to say, but I wish he were still overseas or hospitalized. Worrying about him is easier than having to live with him. When anyone comes to visit, he leaves the house. He's become a vegetarian and won't eat the things he used to love because he can't stand the thought of animals dying to provide him with a meal. He didn't just lose a leg; he lost his mind. I can't deal with it," Rosa had complained.

"Rosa, you need to talk to his psychiatrist or Father O'Mara, the Army chaplain. Maybe one of them can help."

The psychiatrist had responded as she expected—more medication or hospitalization. So, Rosa went to see Father O'Mara before making a decision.

"Rosa, I know a woman who had a similar problem," the priest assured her. "Like you, this poor, frustrated, exhausted woman was searching for an answer. In desperation, she sought the help of a healer who told her, 'I can make a potion that will heal your husband, but it requires a white hair from the chest of a bear.'"

The priest continued his story: "'Where can I get such a hair?' the woman asked.

"The healer told her, 'There's a bear living in a cave on the mountain. If you can get close enough to pluck a white hair from his chest, I can save your husband.'

"So, the woman spent months outside the bear's cave feeding and befriending him. She showed great patience and one day was able to get close enough to pluck a hair from his chest. When the bear reared up in anger, she turned and ran. When she arrived at the healer's house, the healer took the hair and threw it into the fire.

"'You promised me a potion. I risked my life for that hair,'" she cried.

"'Now go home and be as patient with your husband as you were with the bear.'"

Rosa followed the priest's advice, and several months later the townspeople were stunned to see Sal swinging down Main Street. From that morning on, you could set your watch by his daily routine. Every day at seven o'clock he would kiss Rosa good-bye. And regardless of the weather, he'd start swinging down Main Street to the radio station.

The station manager, a former WWII Army buddy of Sal's, knew better than to get in his way. At the station Sal would give his daily weather report: "Today's weather: sunshine, sunshine, sunshine." The hopeful and gentle look of Sal's eyes silenced those who didn't agree with his report.

He then swung over to the green, across from the church, to sit on his accustomed bench, from which he would hold court among the park regulars and passersby, cheerily dispensing good mornings, advice, and opinions. No one dared take his seat or disagree with his weather report. Likewise, his hour of conversing with God—another of his well-practiced routines—was sacrosanct. When it was over, he swung down to the Athenian Diner and hopped up the steps for breakfast, which Spiro always had ready and waiting. Like his weather report it never varied: half a pink grapefruit, a slice of melon, hot oatmeal with raisins, buttered whole wheat cinnamon raisin toast, ginger marmalade, black decaf coffee, and the *Topeka Sentinel*. After breakfast he was off to work at the hardware store.

On Sunday he followed a somewhat different routine. Instead of oatmeal and toast, Spiro had waffles, a blueberry blintz, and syrup waiting. On the way home Sal stopped at the bakery for a half dozen fresh pecan tarts. It was his silent thank you and never-ending love note to Rosa.

Tripod's whine interrupted his daily chat with God—something no human would ever dare. "Sorry, old boy," said Sal, grabbing his crutches. "God and me will have to pick up where we left off tomorrow. Now, let me show you where I work."

Luckily for Sal, his good-hearted boss shared his passion for animals. Tripod was given the run of the store and proved as popular with the customers as Sal, whose how-to expertise on home repair was highly regarded in the community. When the store closed that evening, Sal turned to Tripod and said, "It's time for you to meet the *real* boss."

When Sal introduced Tripod to Rosa, she had to admit the pooch was cute. She dutifully oohed and aahed—then she read her husband the riot act.

"Sal, you ought to call him Minus because you're both missing something, and it's more than a leg."

"Tripod don't worry she has a good heart. You'll see."

"Sal let's get serious. He doesn't have a chance of becoming family unless you agree to my conditions. If you do, he can stay. After my mastectomy you didn't start calling me Flat Busted or introduce me as your single-breasted wife. I won't let you give him a name that makes him less than whole and focuses on what's missing and not who and what he is. He's more than a symbol for you to use. You need to realize you can't change anyone; you can only love and coach them. So, condition number one, you find another name for your foxhole buddy.

"Number two, you start wearing your artificial leg and dump the crutches. Everyone in Topeka has seen you and heard what you have to say. Enough already! It's time you start being complete. We're all wounded, Sal. Lives are healed when we share our wounds, words, and feelings, not by just exposing our deformities. I don't have to bare my chest to help other men and women. I just have to say the word 'cancer' and we all become kindred spirits who understand each other. You want to wear your Purple Heart, fine. But the crutches are out, and the leg is in, or else your buddy goes back to the shelter.

"It's time to show people you are enabled and not disabled. You can't keep living a loss. It's time for you to get a life and become authentic and complete again and turn the curse into a blessing."

As she waited for Sal's response Rosa realized she had come a long way to be able to speak like that and let her heart make up her mind.

"I can't talk about it."

6

"Sal, stop holding it in. Burst the dam and find the energy to move forward."

Rosa embraced him as his past overwhelmed him. Through the tears and sobbing Rosa heard, "I love you, and since you called him my buddy his new name will be Buddy."

"Sal, that's another meaningless name. You need to think of something that will make him unique and special. So, figure it out and then we can discuss it."

After dinner Sal came back into the kitchen. "Okay, I've got some names to discuss with you. The options are Furphy and Sex. You didn't want little pieces of fur in the house so he can be named after them or we can call him Sex. So, which do you like?"

"Sal, you're nuts. Who wouldn't prefer having Sex around the house? But you're insane. I cannot accept a name like that. Sal, we have neighbors."

"Yeah, and when Sex barks at night, and the next day when they complain about it at the supermarket, I can ask them, 'Did you have a problem with Sex last night?' That ought to shut them up. And when I license him, I can ask the town clerk if I need a license for Sex if I just have Sex on my property. And I can have Sex at work, and if he ever bites anyone and we end up in court, I can ask the judge to have Sex for a week and see how he feels after that."

"Sal, you are a basket case."

"Honey, it's a done deal. I've had Sex for one day and he's already got me smiling and the two of us talking. So, Sex it is. Let's open a bottle of wine and celebrate having Sex."

Sal and Sex became inseparable, cutting a distinctive figure about town. Rosa pointedly called the dog Furphy in public, while Sal never tired of the shock value inherent in introducing his three-legged companion as Sex. Spiro even made an exception to his no pets' rule, knowing you served both or lost two customers. Each morning he made a few wisecracks about having Sex in the diner and had a meaty snack waiting under the table for the doggie, who was not a vegetarian.

Rosa, however, knew that discipline was an important part of training a dog, no matter how Sal pleaded with her about letting Sex sleep with them. "I have no problem with you spending more time with the dog than you do with me, but our bed is off limits," she stated flatly. "There will be only the real thing in our bed."

A few weeks later Sal was late getting home from a veterans meeting. When Rosa started to get ready for bed, Sex was snoozing with his head on Sal's pillow.

"I have to admit, you're a plus, not a minus. You can stay until your Daddy gets home. Hey, having Sex in bed tonight could be fun."

When Sex didn't greet him at the front door Sal went to the bedroom and found his two loved ones curled up on the bed. He gently awakened Rosa with tears in his eyes, "Rosa, bless you for your love and acceptance."

"Honey, we're both learning."

As they embraced, Sex's snoring startled them.

Rosa burst out laughing. "Now you know what I go through sleeping with you."

When Rosa awakened the next morning, seeing Sex nestled in the empty space provided by Sal's amputation made her abundantly aware he was a plus in their lives.

CHAPTER 2

Sunday morning found Danny Hoffman still in his pajamas, half-listening to the top forty countdown on the radio on his nightstand. Elvis, Sinatra, and Crosby crooned while his cat, Penny, the only creature besides his mom he felt comfortable with, purred contentedly beside him on the bed. Every now and then the high school senior's attention strayed to the composition book, open on his belly, on which he'd scrawled his tortured thoughts the restless night before.

"Danny, honey, breakfast's ready!" Mom shouted from the kitchen. "I'll be leaving for church in a minute. Want to come?"

Danny shouted back: "I have to write a letter for Mr. Schultz to put in the *Sentinel*."

"You can write it later. Come on, you'll feel better."

"Mom, I don't feel comfortable around people."

"Honey, stop judging yourself."

"I'll get the letter done and see you later. Love you."

Mom suddenly appeared in the doorway of Danny's bedroom. The teen reflexively sat up in bed, discreetly closing the comp book in the same motion.

"All this shouting back and forth is for the birds," said Mom, whisking off her apron. "I'm not going to force you to come but I do insist that you keep your appointment with Dr. Karl tomorrow. I'm sure he can help you."

"Okay, okay, we'll talk later."

"Someday you'll understand what blessings are and find meaning in all this. God is forgiving. No one is blaming you. Dad's death taught me more than all my years as a social worker have. Danny, you can abandon your past, or learn from it. The one thing you can't do is change it."

With an exasperated groan Danny fell back on the bed; the impact sent Penny scurrying. "Yeah, yeah, Mom, I've heard all this before. I know you mean well, but—"

"How about a picnic later? Being outside might help."

"Okay, okay. If that'll make you happy."

"Danny, don't you understand? It's *your* happiness I want." She stood there for an awkward moment before adding: "Your breakfast is on the stove. Pancakes. Better eat them while they're hot."

Danny's mom closed the door before she lost control of her emotions. She stepped outside into the autumn air's crisp, clean embrace, while the vibrant foliage dazzled her eyes. On this October Sunday the earth felt like a sanctuary and walking to church a part of the service. She hoped the beauty of the day would lift Danny's spirits. Nothing else seemed to be able to.

Upon arriving at the church Martha followed the graveled path to her husband's grave in the adjoining cemetery. Kneeling on the kerchief she pulled from her purse, she placed a single flower on the headstone—a yellow chrysanthemum plucked from a planter on her front porch.

"Gil, Danny feels he's to blame, not only for your death, but for all the pain and suffering everyone feels due to the loss of a loved one. Please help him to see that he is a beloved child of God."

Closing her eyes, she clasped her hands together prayerfully. "Dear Jesus, give us the strength to go on and find a way to fulfill thy will in the midst of our pain. Help us to see that we can be saved. Help us to live as you did. Please take Danny's hand and help him to find faith and know that his sins are forgiven."

When she finished conversing with her savior and her husband, she took out a mirror, corrected the damage caused by her tears, tucked the kerchief into her purse and walked to the church. Like others in their small church community, she had her special seat, hers next to the window overlooking Gil's grave. She prayed silently while listening to the choir, wishing Danny was with her.

As soon as his mom left the house Danny went to the kitchen. He lifted the towel covering the short stack of pancakes in a Pyrex dish on the table, releasing the tempting aroma. Having no appetite, he recovered the dish, but did take a sip of the orange juice Mom had poured for him. Spying the dirty skillet in the sink, he felt compelled to wash it. *The least I can do*, he thought, *in return for all she's done for me.*

Next, he went to his dad's old desk and began writing on a fresh page in his composition book.

To The Greatest Mom In The World,

I'm sorry but I can't look in the mirror without remembering. I feel guilty. I have hurt so many people by what I have done even though I was trying to help and not hurt them. I'm wounded and scarred inside and out and know what Mr. Roget meant when he said he was tired. I don't have the courage to choose life. I'll be with Dad and I won't hurt anymore. You're the greatest and I love you, but I don't have your faith. I know you'll forgive me even if God doesn't.

Let Dr. Karl help you, Mom. I can't find peace and forgiveness here. There's only one way I know of to stop hurting. Death will be my healing.

Please put on my headstone: Together Forever. Thanks for your love—I can take it with me.

Mom, you and Penny were my life. Please love her and care for her and let her be your new child. She was my Penny from Heaven. Let her be yours too.

Your Son,
Danny

The letter to Mr. Schultz, who oversaw all submitted columns and letters to the editor of the *Sentinel*, asked the townspeople for their forgiveness too. When he finished the letters, Danny placed them on the table in the front hall, went back upstairs and opened his bedroom window. The sun-drenched oaks and maples lining the street were draped in crazy quilts of orange, gold, and red. It was a beautiful day to die.

He pulled his Sunday best out of the closet and dressed quickly. Before the fire he looked just like his dad. It was hard to tell from old photographs which one you were looking at. Both were six-foot, blue eyed, curly haired blonds. But now his face was a scarred, cruel caricature of that kinship. He fought to hold back the tears, recalling the day of the fire and his dad's death.

He returned to the den, pocketed two shotgun shells, created a harness out of belts and hung the rifle down his back between his shoulders. He slipped into a loose-fitting coat to conceal the rifle and stepped out onto the porch. Penny ran out before the door closed. He scooped the tabby up and hugged her to his chest. "Can't have you following me, sweet girl," he said, kissing the top of Penny's head before placing her back inside. From a window Penny watched him trudging down the driveway, her eyes wide with curiosity. Danny paused to turn around and mouth a goodbye.

"Penny don't feel bad I was going to take you because you give me love and strength, but I couldn't treat you that way. I love you too much to leave you on your own. Let our last moment be a pleasant memory."

Danny had expected grief to dull his senses. Instead he felt as if he were seeing things for the first time. Maybe our Creator was an artist for whom time didn't exist, but until he could understand why, dying was less painful than living.

He adjusted the rifle and started walking. As he passed the town green, he felt drawn to Sal, as usual sitting on his favorite bench. Sex capered about, excited about the approaching company.

"Morning, Mr. Petonito."

"It is a g-o-o-o-d morning, Danny." Sal invited him to sit with a wave of his hand. Danny nodded but did not sit or bend to pet Sex; the rifle encumbered his movements. Danny hoped Sal wouldn't sense anything unusual and spoke quickly to avoid being questioned.

"Mr. Petonito, what are you and Sex doing today?"

"We don't plan ahead. Every day's a new experience."

Danny had long admired Sal's rosy outlook on life. Here he was, the one-legged town character and treasure with every reason to be embittered, but he always listened and had a kind word for everyone he met. Danny couldn't stop his own pessimism from slipping out.

"I just can't understand how God could let things happen the way they do."

"Still beating yourself up about the fire, I see. Danny, a perfect world would be meaningless—a magic trick with nothing for us to do or learn. People need to learn from their wounds and become wounded healers and teachers, serving love, rather than hiding their wounds. If everything were perfect, we'd all go nuts. If the pain leads you to create a new life, it's a labor pain and worth having."

"I'm sure you've heard it all from your mom. What you've experienced ought to be a reminder of how uncertain life is. Life is about beginnings. Don't let your past hold you back and don't waste the best days of your life, Danny. Today is always our best day so live and enjoy it. If you ever want to talk you know where to find me."

"Mr. Petonito, I'd..."

Sal burst into tears as Danny stepped forward.

Embarrassed by his tears, Sal motioned for Danny to wait as Sex jumped onto the bench and began licking his face. Sal held him against his chest, rubbed his nose against the terrier's, and broke into a smile.

"See what I mean, Danny? Only God knows why, but I do know that life is about love. Go touch someone's life. You'll see. Did you want to ask me something?"

"No, not really. It's just ... I don't know where you find the strength to go on. I just want you to know how much I admire you, and I want to thank you for all that you've taught me and done for us. You are a role model for us all."

"Danny, I've sat here for a lot of years and some people enjoy my company, some avoid me, some go by in silence and some in tears. Some make speeches, proclaiming me a hero, or offer their condolences, but you're the first person to ever thank me. How people react to me says more about what's in them than in me. It was for you I went to war."

Danny managed a little smile. He thought of saying "I appreciate your service," but he knew how trite that could sound, especially to a vet like Sal.

"You are so smart. I guess I do have a question for you, Mr. Petonito. What's your motto? What's your philosophy on life?"

"Danny, understand why, imitate how, and know when. That's it."

Danny puzzled a moment over the cryptic advice. "Uh, thanks, Mr. Petonito. See you around."

"Take it easy, kid." As the boy walked away, he noticed that his gait was unusually stiff, and there was an odd bulge on his back.

Danny turned to enter the church cemetery, wishing he could understand Sal and God better.

"Hi, Danny."

Danny stopped along the graveled path at the greeting from his classmate. His hand darted self-consciously to his face in a vain attempt to hide the scars.

"Hi, Bev, I didn't see you. How come you're not inside?"

"I couldn't bring myself to go inside on such a beautiful day. I'm waiting for my mom so we can walk home together. Why aren't you with your mom?"

"I need some time alone. She understands. I have something I need to take care of at my dad's grave."

"I'm sorry about everything, Danny. I hope you feel better soon. When you're ready maybe we can go to a movie or something. I'd really like to help. I used to blame myself, too, and keep all my feelings inside."

"Thanks, I just can't talk now." He stalked away, feeling Bev's eyes burning into the back of his head.

Meeting Bev started him thinking again and compelled him to look at the headstones for some last words that might help him make sense of it all.

"If I could just be God for a day maybe I'd understand why."

He felt responsible for two deaths and now a third. For the first time he realized he had to be willing to end his own life; that would take all the guts he had, and then some, but he didn't see how he could live in peace. What would his dad tell him to do? Maybe he should talk to Dr. Karl first. His thinking stopped when he came to the grave.

He knew his mom had been there from the flower. He slipped the rifle from beneath his coat, inserted a shell, leaned back against the headstone and rested the warm muzzle against his forehead. He recalled picking out his dad's headstone. He and Mom wanted everyone to know how precious each moment of Dad's life had been. He ran his fingers over the epitaph's etched characters: His Life Taught Us How To Live and His Death How To Die. Gilbert Hoffman, 41 years 6 months 15 days. Died July 11, 1954.

"God, I know You talk to people. So why don't You or my Dad talk to me? The only thing I've done is hurt people. I need another life. What they do after

I'm gone is up to them. I just want to stop hurting and be forgiven. I can't understand what needs to die and what needs to live anymore."

The rifle slipped from his hands, snapping him out of his reverie. He cried, remembering the times he and his Dad went hunting together.

"Mom, I know I shouldn't do this but I'm tired, tired of hurting. Death is my gift. I'll be unalive, perfect, free and with Dad again. Living hurts too much. There isn't anything worse than hurting people you love. My mistakes have been the cause of so much suffering. God, do you understand me?"

He recalled his mom's constant answer: "Don't question. Let your faith sustain you. Problems are God's redirections." It didn't help now. It never had.

"I'm praying for a new life and a chance to start again. Do You really love us or is my mom just saying that? I don't know where You are, or if You even exist. My mom believes in 'Thy will be done' and 'not why me but try me,' but I don't have the strength she has. I know You make deals, so I don't have anything to lose. I'm no lawyer so I'll make it simple. You may be merciful and just, as my mom says, but I need a sign.

"You gave us Ten Commandments, so I'll give You ten minutes and then I'm going to pull the trigger. I have my faults but I'm not a bad person. I love You and if I'm Your child, like my mom says, then forgive me. I need forgiveness more than understanding. They tell me what I remember You are willing to forget and forgive."

Danny took off his dad's wristwatch and rested it on his leg. It was time to disconnect from his life and memories. The motion of the second hand reminded him of Sal's leg swinging in rhythm as he swung along on his crutches. A centipede climbed onto his arm. He was about to brush it off, but was entranced by its rhythmic movements, and let it walk across his hand.

"You're so perfect. I bet you never hurt anyone. You did a good job creating this little guy. I guess You do love all your creatures, and maybe You do love me, but I sure could use a sign. Maybe if we changed places for a minute but that's never going to happen. So..."

The centipede walked up the barrel as the choir began singing its closing hymn.

"Thanks, God. Bye, Mom."

Danny again pressed the muzzle against his forehead and squeezed the trigger, just the way his dad had taught him. For the first time since his Dad's death, he felt loved, forgiven, unalive, and perfect.

Martha sat in the church pew, wishing Danny could hear the choir sing 'And though it makes Him sad to see the way we live, He'll always say, I forgive.'

"I'll sing this for him this afternoon when I get home," she thought.

At the sound of the gunshot Martha looked out the church window and fell to her knees, screaming Danny's name. The choir stopped singing. The parishioners rose in their seats. Bev started running towards the grave. Sal recalled painful memories. The centipede walked unhurriedly back to its nest to resume this tragic comedy we call life.

CHAPTER 3

D r. Jonathan Hokmah sat at his desk organizing his papers while thinking about how hectic the next few weeks were going to be. First the move to Middletown, Connecticut, to take on the job of chief psychiatrist at Peaceful Acres, a residential therapy center, and the following week attending the American Psychiatric Association meeting in San Francisco. He knew his decision to relocate his practice and move was the right thing to do because the excessive time he devoted to his private practice was having a deleterious effect on his marriage and family.

He was mature enough to accept the fact that he had become a psychiatrist because of his own problems. Particularly the feelings of failure his childhood had generated; his mother had effectively committed suicide by ignoring her breast cancer and his father drank himself to death after telling Jon he didn't love him enough to want to live.

His wounds had taught him to respond to his gnawing unrest in the same way one satisfies the pangs of hunger, by finding ways to nourish one's life. He had learned to let his patients express themselves freely, knowing that their stories and not their diagnosis revealed the truth. He listened to his patients until they heard their true story from themselves and knew what they needed to do to resolve the problem. This gave them a chance to hear about their own woundedness and start the process of transformation—far better than him prescribing a pill.

Hokmah was not your average psychiatrist. He had learned how to use aggression in a disciplined way as a former linebacker at Penn State. His imposing size, dark chocolate skin, shaved head, and piercing gaze made patients and staff alike feel like they were in the presence of a black bear. And when they heard him speak in a basso profundo voice, they knew from his erudition he was a cuddly and intellectual bruin, not a ferocious one.

The flashing light on his desk, announcing the arrival of his next patient, interrupted his thoughts. He glanced at the record to be sure he had the correct name, and then opened his office door to find three men sitting in the waiting room. Two were muscular, well-dressed young men while the third, a distinguished looking older man, projected an aura of authority and power. His eyes, concealed behind sunglasses, revealed nothing while observing everything. His hair and mustache, lightly peppered with gray, were neatly trimmed. He wore an impeccably tailored double-breasted Saint Laurent suit. It was obvious he was moneyed and liked to flaunt the fact.

"Mr. Birsamatto, I'm Dr. Jonathan Hokmah. Feel free to call me by my first name."

They shook hands. "Thank you, Jonathan. I prefer first names as well. So please call me Carmine. These are my associates, Michael and Gabriel."

The young hulks nodded almost imperceptibly. Carmine motioned to them to remain seated and followed Hokmah into the consultation room, where the doctor seated himself behind his desk, and Carmine settled into the chair in front of him, taking some care not to wrinkle the flaps of his jacket.

"Carmine, I want to help you so my first question is not what's your chief complaint but what is the story you bring with you and how can I help you?"

"I've heard you're an unusual shrink who hugs his patients but that's not why I'm here. I presume you know who I am and what I do for a living. So, I'll get right to the point. First, I want to make it clear I don't deny I'm a racketeer but I'm not a thug. You were recommended to me as someone I could talk to. You need to understand I'm not some character in a gangster movie or TV-14 cop show procedural. I expect to be treated with the same sense of professionalism you show all your patients."

"Certainly, Carmine. Your past is not a problem; I'm here to help you, not judge you. Tell me your story and what you're looking for, and I'll do my best to help."

"I'll start from the beginning, so you'll understand where I'm coming from. It all goes back to my teenage years. My dad was a landscaper and wanted me to work with him, but his workaholic lifestyle never appealed to me. He was going day and night. All year long people drove him nuts; between mowing and planting shrubs and laying sod, he never took a vacation. The neighbors rather looked down on us because my pop was always filthy, and our yard was littered with landscaping equipment.

"Now, on the other hand, my grandfather was a businessman. He dressed well and he spoke well. You might say he cultivated a certain elegance. I liked how the neighbors treated him. How the hell was I to know he was treated that way because people feared him? He was an honest-to God Mafioso—real *Godfather* stuff. But the more I saw of him and studied how he interacted with people, the more impressed I was. He was the one I admired and when I was old enough, I started working for him.

"Working for my grandfather was different. He was a professional and treated everyone with respect. Not all this 'fuck you' stuff you see on TV. And he expected me to be a gentleman. Did he do some things that bothered me, and am I troubled by some of the things I've done? Yes, and that's the reason why, after all these years, I'm here. I don't feel comfortable doing this anymore. People I talk to can't believe me or think I'm nuts to want to change my life, so

I need professional help. Someone I can talk to about things and in ways I can't talk to the people I work with, or with my family.

"I feel a need to change. I know how to walk away from the old life, but I don't know how to begin a new one. You know, like disengaging and creating a new engagement in my life and not a termination or retirement. I want to disengage, not retire.

"I have so many things in the works, all organized by the old Carmine, that I need to complete or let go of to start a new and meaningful life. I need to become a grandfather and quit being a godfather. I've got a great wife who supports my decision. There's more to my story but that's it in a nutshell. You're the only person, besides my wife, I've discussed this with. Can we do this? Are you willing to help me? If you're worried about my business connections being a problem, don't be. Also, finances are not an issue. I need to know if you can be there for me and that what we share stays here."

"Carmine, my answer is yes but as I told you over the phone, I will be going away for at least a week. What I'd like to do is see you again in two weeks and see how the two of us hit it off before I make a long-term decision. I'll be moving to my new office in Middletown. Are you willing to drive up there?"

"Sure, Doc."

"Okay, then let's set up an appointment and go from there."

As Hokmah scanned his calendar he was startled when his desk light started flashing. He hadn't scheduled the next appointment until well after Carmine's, to avoid him meeting anyone in the waiting room.

"Carmine, I hate to bring this up, but do you want to leave through my private entrance to avoid meeting anyone?" He added quickly, "For your own privacy, of course."

Carmine flashed a barracuda smile. "I would, Doc, but the boys are waiting for me."

Hokmah handed Carmine his appointment card, then opened the door to the waiting room. A man whose expression and jittery movements reminded Hokmah of a frightened squirrel sprang to his feet as they entered. George Dingfelder, a Jewish physician with a name longer than his lean body, stood before them, a nervous smile on his angular face.

"I can't believe it. This must be a sign. Mr. Birsamatto, you're one of the reasons I decided to see a psychiatrist. You sure look younger and slimmer in person than on TV."

Carmine burst out laughing. "Saw me on the evening news, did you?" he said, slapping him on the back and knocking him forward a good two feet. Hokmah, despite his training, was at a loss for words.

"Dr. Dingfelder, your appointment isn't until three."

"I came early to go over what I wanted to say so I would get my case history right the first time. Mr. Birsamatto, I didn't mean to be impolite. I apologize. Perhaps I can be of service to you some day. Here's my card if you ever need a consultation."

"George, go and sit down in my office please."

As George left the room, Carmine and Hokmah shook hands again.

"Who's that character?" Carmine asked.

"You know as much as I do. It's his first visit and it looks like I have an interesting afternoon ahead of me."

"Good luck, Doc. Be seeing you." He jerked his head at his associates and the trio left, leaving in their wake the scent of Man by Jimmy Choo.

When Hokmah went into his office he found George sitting in the patient's chair, gnawing on his fingernails. Hokmah resumed his place behind his desk.

"I let my patients call me by my first name if that makes them comfortable. I'd like another minute to review the notes I made about the information you sent."

"Doc, I have a photographic memory. I can repeat what I sent and save you time."

There was no point in trying to treat George like a normal patient. Hokmah leaned back and motioned for George to begin.

"I'm a thirty-seven-year-old, white, Jewish, male, physician in good physical condition. My first marriage ended in divorce after three years. I have a ten-year-old son from that marriage. Five years ago, I remarried. My present wife is the sister of my surgical partner. She had one daughter, now age seven, by her previous marriage. Her first husband died in an auto accident. I adopted her daughter and three years ago we had a daughter of our own.

"I am the sole support of my first wife and child, as well as my present family. They have no significant resources. So, my financial obligations have kept me in a state of constant turmoil. I'll admit I'm extremely conscientious and borderline obsessive-compulsive, but I like to do things right. It's my surgical personality.

"I was a cross-country runner in college and my one therapeutic activity is jogging. I deal with stress by running away from it. If I don't find time to run, I become more anxious. Running and going to medical conferences are therapeutic.

"I'm not on any medications and not a great believer in therapy because of my past experience. Our marriage counselor was a divorced woman who couldn't make her marriage work. So how was she going to help me? It was two against one at every session. I got tired of defending myself and shelling out the bucks with no results.

"Let me explain what broke the camel's back. There's a room in our house I use as an office. My desk, computer, and papers are there. The kids are not to touch anything without my permission. My wife thinks I'm obsessive about it, but she doesn't understand how important my time is. I don't want anything misplaced. I have more faith that things will be where I left them when I'm in a hotel than when I'm home.

"The room opens on a fenced-in patio, through a sliding glass door so I have a nice view and connects through a hallway to our master bedroom and bathroom. It helps me relax to look out at nature. I have a pet door so my dogs can visit me or go outside. My wife placed her cats' litter boxes in one corner of the room, without asking me. They go in and out that way too. I noticed cats in your yard, so you'll understand. The dogs are my pets and responsibility and the cats are hers, but when one of them uses the litter box while I'm trying to work, I've got to stop and clean it. Who can work with that smell? And my wife smokes, which upsets the hell out of me. I've asked her a million times to stop but she never really tries to. What's even crazier, she smokes outdoors to avoid exposing her cats to the smoke. With my luck she'll get asthma or cancer and I'll be left with her cats. You can see what thinking about her does to me. The other day the local paper ran a story about a man who shot his wife and then committed suicide. The police said they couldn't find a motive. The policeman investigating the case obviously wasn't married."

Hokmah, struggling to maintain his clinical detachment, had to bite his tongue to stifle a chuckle.

"The other night I'm sitting at my desk finishing up reading some papers about a patient I have to see early the next day. I have to drive to the hospital so I'm anxious to get washed up and into bed. I hear a *Jeopardy* rerun playing in the bedroom. My wife's addicted to the program. So, I figure I can use the bathroom and then get to bed. When I walk into the dressing area the bathroom door's closed and locked.

"We have another bathroom but it's between the kid's rooms and I don't want to wake them. Besides, all my stuff's in the bathroom my wife's in. So, I ask, 'Honey, can I come in?' By the way, my wife's name is Barbara, but her family nicknamed her Honey. When she was two, she knocked a jar of honey off the kitchen counter and the honey ended up all over her. The family heard her crying and found her sitting in a puddle of honey with the dogs licking her.

"Anyway, I say, 'Honey, I need to get into the bathroom. I have a case I need to see early in the morning, and I want to get to bed.'

"'I'm getting ready to go to bed, too,' she yells back. 'I'll be out in a few minutes.'

"'Why is the TV on?' I ask her.

"'Because I'm going back in the bedroom.'

"'But you're not there now and electricity costs money,' I argued. 'How many times do I have to tell you to turn the TV, lights, and hot water off when you leave a room? Do I have to hang a sign on the bathroom door? When we go on vacation, we don't leave things on because we're coming home again.'

"'Then put a TV in the bathroom,' she says. Doc, are you married?"

"Yes, George, I am."

"Thank God, then you know how crazy it gets. The same nonsense day after day. Women, they're always getting ready, never on time. Our bathroom looks like a drugstore after a bomb went off in the cosmetics and pharmacy departments. Hell, I'm lucky if I can find my shaving stuff half the time. Sleeping with cats, sex with them watching, water running, plus lights on. Locked out of the bathroom and the smell of cigarettes. For dinner, microwave, eat out, or takeout.

"Well, this particular time I was tired and damn mad and let her know it. I didn't care who I woke up. When I get angry, she tells me that I have peccadilloes, too, that she has to live with, like putting tomatoes in the fridge, eating and walking too fast, and shortcomings like not helping with the housework. Sometimes she'll make me feel guilty for my anger by saying, 'You're upsetting the pets' when I bellow. The remark that really gets me is, 'You're so handsome when you're angry.' I can never tell if she's serious or just trying to get my goat. She never wants to talk seriously about my problems.

"It's hopeless. So, I go back into my office and sit down. I turn on the TV to watch the eleven o'clock news and calm down. You know how a war or a terrorist bombing takes your mind off your troubles. That's why I was so shocked to see Birsamatto. He's coming out of the courthouse and the reporter's saying how the judge had thrown out his case on some technicality. He went on and on about how he seemed to have led a charmed life, never being convicted of anything. I didn't get his name at the time, but I got a good look at him.

"I read the papers. I know what goes on in the world. I've read *The Godfather*. I've watched *The Sopranos* and seen *Analyze This*. I thought maybe God was using the TV and now your office to send me a message. No coincidences. Doc cut out the weird look. I wasn't serious about it. I'd never consider killing anyone, much less my wife, but fantasizing about it sure made me feel better. It seemed like a natural thing to do for a guy in my situation. I felt much better, like I was self-medicating myself with fantasy. I could even write a book about it and make money because of my problems.

"I know it sounds sick, but I resented my wives for making my life hell. I felt trapped and powerless. It may sound crazy to talk this way, but a divorce means more problems while a well-orchestrated disappearance solves everything. Remember, with two wives all your problems are multiplied, and you learn how short a month is when you pay alimony. I understand that marriage is a struggle and an ordeal; it's about a relationship and not personal desires. But I can't see any other solution if my wife won't accept that we have a problem and see a counselor with me. The only choice left seemed to be you eliminate your wife, yourself, or your marriage to be free.

"As crazy as it sounds, fantasizing about my options made me feel better. I knew it wasn't realistic, but my thinking was a mess, so I felt better imagining a solution to my troubles. Adam and Eve didn't hit it off either but eventually worked it out. Honey reminds me of Eve. It's never her fault. There's always a figurative serpent to blame. I know that I decide how I feel but there's a limit to what I can deal with, and surgeons are used to cutting cancers out.

"How do you have a positive attitude when you can't afford another divorce and my surgical partner is my wife's brother? He's the one I have to thank for bringing us together. He introduced us at a medical convention. Honey's face immediately attracted me and helps me put up with her. I was lonely and too dumb to think it all out and so was Honey. She was having her own troubles after her first husband died. The next thing you know we're married, and my troubles are just beginning. I felt like that old Woody Allen quote: 'One path leads to despair and utter hopelessness. The other, to total extinction. Let us pray we have the wisdom to choose correctly.'

"My wives and kids are well insured. I'm not a cruel guy so I started fantasizing about how I could do this in a nice way. You know, like creating a movie or writing a book in my mind. I don't want to hurt anybody; I just want some peace.

"I know it's sick, but you have no idea how desperate I was. Fantasizing helped me stop feeling like a victim and daydreaming is not a crime. Don't tell me you've never done it, Doc."

Hokmah tapped a pencil against his lips, his face a noncommittal study. George continued.

"Okay, so now I was writing the script. I have two brothers. One's a lawyer, but I didn't want him to start acting like my therapist. The other brother runs a body shop and does auto restorations. If she could have an accident, and if she were giving my first wife a ride at the time? Wow...great plot, right? I figured I'd hang out with my younger brother and learn about cars. I felt much better. I wasn't the victim anymore. I had a plan, like something I would present to a patient with cancer.

"When Honey came out of the bathroom she was surprised at the change. Believe me, over the next few months I felt more in control of my future. I started to write it all down. I know a lot of married guys who would go for the book and make me some money. And I read that keeping a journal of your feelings is therapeutic too.

"Now I had a hobby that took my mind off my troubles. I couldn't tell anyone why I felt better but they were happy to see the change. Whenever things would get me down, I would imagine being a free man with the cats given to the animal shelter. No cat poop. No money problems. It was great therapy. I didn't feel trapped anymore. Fantasizing really helped. Like meditation.

"I hung out with my brother whenever I could. I would jog over to his garage for a cup of coffee and learn about the things you had to be careful about in auto restorations: brakes, wiring, transmission, exhaust, seat belts—all the things that involved safety and not just the car's appearance. It's like learning about all the body's anatomical parts. I told him I was seeing a lot of accident cases and wanted to have a better understanding of liability issues and the repair costs involved. He was glad to see me take an interest in his work because he and I had never been that close. I had more in common with my older brother. We were the thinkers and my younger brother was the mechanical one. He was always building or fixing things and laughing at us for being so helpless. I have no sisters and no experience growing up with women.

"I remembered reading about the wives of the Mafia big shots starting the car every morning to be sure no bomb had been hooked up to the ignition system. Boy, that's love for you. If the car doesn't blow up, hubby comes out, kisses his wife goodbye and goes to work.

"Life is looking more hopeful. I have choices now. Honey's giving me more material for my book and I'm making notes about her. Everyone is pleased that I'm less moody and not obsessing about Honey's behavior. I'm getting more referrals. I'm good at what I do and care about my patients. I do a lot of children's surgery. They teach me more about life than my family. They don't store it up inside."

Hokmah rocked forward in his chair. "George, you're a master storyteller, but enough already. I have other appointments. Can you tell me specifically your reason for coming? How can I help you?"

"I'm getting to that, Doc. I don't like feeling trapped and helpless, or that my happiness depends on fantasies. Last week I lost it again and Honey said, 'George, you're upsetting the animals.' That convinced me I needed to see a shrink. Even I know I need help when my bellowing scares my dogs and when God sends me the Mafia as a sign. I'm getting worried about my thinking. I don't want to hurt anyone."

"George, you should be concerned. Every fantasy is connected to reality and creating your future. I'll be away for two weeks but will see you the week after to discuss more specifically how I can help, and you can decide what you want to do."

"That's great. By the way, what are your cats' names? I came up with some clever names for my pets if I do say so myself. The cat's names are logical and related to my surgical practice: Disability, Hernia, Accident, and Malpractice. The kids renamed them Dizzy Billy, Hernietta, Sid, and Mal. My dogs are Codeine, Valium, and Marijuana. The kids call them Cody, Val, and Mary."

Hokmah found George irritating but warmed to the subject of pets. "My cats have symbolic names. Miracle to remind me of our potential. Penny was inspired by pennies from Heaven and by the mottoes 'Liberty' and 'In God We Trust.' Dickens is a little devil and Gabriel the angel to give us balance. They remind me that if God is at your front door; the Devil is at your back door."

"Pretty good, Doc. Say, could I bring my dogs to our therapy sessions, and do you ever see patients outdoors? You look fit. Could we talk while out jogging or walking?"

"Why do you ask?"

"Well, the dogs help me to relax, and I think about things when I'm running, I wouldn't think about indoors. It's like a meditation for me. Sometimes it's what I see as I run, like how nature handles problems. Nature doesn't have to become strong at the broken places. It knows how to survive."

"Interesting point of view, George. I happen to enjoy personal reflection while I'm jogging too. It has physical and psychological benefits. Most therapeutic."

"And you can protect the environment by picking up cans and bottles for recycling. And—"

"George, we can talk about the practical benefits of recycling next time. We need to finish up."

"Okay, thanks for being so patient."

"I'm here to listen and hopefully guide you through your difficulties and help you to heal." Hokmah paused. "There is something you can do to help your relationship before our next session. It helped my marriage."

Squirrely George danced in his seat. "What is it? Tell me!"

"Install motion detectors on all your lights and appliances so they will go on as Honey enters a room and off when she leaves."

"Why didn't I think of that? Could you write me a prescription? Maybe I can get them covered by insurance and save money on therapy."

"George, we're all multiple personalities but there's hope for you if you still have a childlike character with a sense of humor within you. This week quit fantasizing and work on waking up that kid. Try to act like the man you want to be and keep rehearsing until you get it right. We'll talk more at your next appointment. Just one prescription I want you to fill. Refrain from trying to improve anyone except yourself."

George grinned. "Pretty clever, Doc. Guess that's why you make the big bucks, right?"

"I have one more therapeutic suggestion," said Dr. Hokmah. "When in doubt ask yourself: WWLD?"

"What does that mean?"

"What Would Lassie Do?"

CHAPTER 4

Hokmah's stature and size had the Peaceful Acres staff and patients feeling uncomfortable until the afternoon they saw him on the front porch of his house, wrapped only in a towel, bellowing, "Miracle, Miracle, Miracle!"

When he noticed members of his staff staring at him, he explained drugs and sex had nothing to do with his behavior. He and his wife had an afternoon appointment, and when his wife Judy yelled to him in the shower, "Jon, I can't find the cat anywhere and we need to get going," he jumped out and created the spectacle everyone witnessed, which made them all family.

At the next staff meeting he commented, "Judy and I have four cats. In case you hear me calling out their names it means either Judy or I are looking for them. But if you hear me yell 'Oh, shit,' it means I hit my bald head on something." The rest of the week things went a bit more smoothly.

———✳———

Meanwhile, George felt a bit more hopeful after his visit with Hokmah. After all, how many psychiatrists had a sense of humor? That afternoon he did something squirrels don't often do. He took the time to climb into his hammock and stretch out in the sun.

Honey called from the doorway: "George, did you put on your sunscreen?"

"Yes, dear."

Despite his past experience with therapists, George looked forward to future sessions. Maybe it wasn't healthy to try and be normal. It probably meant you felt inadequate to begin with. As he lay on the hammock his inner voices started their internal dialogue again. He responded with explanations, as if he were in therapy.

"Hell, the way he names his pets is pathological. And why cut me off about picking up empty cans and bottles when I'm out jogging? Squirrels collect acorns. What's wrong with cleaning up the environment and using the deposits to buy lottery tickets? If I win, I can help a lot of animals to be rescued.

"And we need to talk about traffic lights too. They have rhythm. If a light turns green when I jog up to an intersection, or I find a penny from Heaven, I'm in harmony with the universe. There are no coincidences."

George's jogging made him a local celebrity. His neighbors avoided eye contact when they saw him out collecting, and the clerk at the supermarket couldn't figure him out when he showed up with bags full of cans and bottles for recycling. He didn't look like the average homeless person.

He was used to people asking him for directions while he was jogging but one morning when two police cars pulled up next to him, he was scared out of his wits. Seems some lady called in about this guy running away from her house with a bag full of stolen items. Of course, they were George's bag of cans and bottles. After some tense moments, George ultimately convinced the cops he wasn't a felon but rather an eminent surgeon who just happened to feel strongly about environmental issues.

The voices continued their dialogue. "I wish I could choose my relatives the way we choose pets. My labs are like tranquilizers and, although I hate to admit it, the cats have helped a time or two.

"Cats in the bedroom upset me until they started to curl up next to me, or stretched out on my chest, purring contentedly. Their soft, warm fur became my security blanket and helped me fall asleep unless they stepped on my bladder. What has impressed me is that they seemed to intuitively know when I needed attention. Thinking about my pets helps me to relax—something Honey seems incapable of doing. She's always making lists, going shopping, feeding the kids or the animals, watching TV, going to the doctor or dentist, in the bathroom or doing the laundry.

"We'd have a better relationship if Honey treated me like a cat and I treated her like a dog. Maybe I ought to apply to veterinary school. I'll have to talk to our vet about a career change and find out if the people who bring the pets in take the joy out of it."

His thoughts were interrupted by Honey calling to ask about the sunscreen again.

As he dutifully applied the sunscreen, he thought she really does care about me and I should probably start acting like the husband she needs.

CHAPTER 5

Every summer Carmine and his wife Maria rented the same house in East Orleans, on Cape Cod, and invited their eight grandchildren, who didn't put him on a pedestal, to join them. Carmine was at peace on Cape Cod. The rhythmic roar of the waves felt sacred and touched something deep inside him. Every night he would sit for hours, often alone, listening. He felt a special connection to water; its ability to change form taught him invaluable lessons about life and surviving difficulties.

Everything happening through immersion, and the still pond allowing you to see your reflection and know your true self, he realized, were all part of what brought him to Hokmah. The more he thought about water the more it became his therapist. Even when water encountered an obstructing rock it found a way around it while making healing sounds—a far cry from what people did when they ran into trouble.

His afternoons were spent on the sands of Nauset Beach watching his grandchildren playing in the surf. His grandchildren brought out Carmine's wolf like pack behavior more than his business relationships. He thanked God for them. They were great critics and had no fear of telling him how they felt. They knew he cared, criticized him freely, and polished his mirror.

The time with his grandchildren gave him the freedom he needed to think things out. He knew that what he shared in therapy, as long as it didn't endanger or threaten the lives of others, was privileged information. And maybe it wasn't a coincidence George showed up when he did. He had been looking for a medical doctor to use in a business enterprise and help him retire with a few extra bucks. George could be the perfect candidate for the job. He'd have his associates check him out.

Carmine Jr. interrupted his reverie. "Poppie, come down to the water with us."

The kids were like flowers to him, each one different and beautiful in their own way, bending in the wind one moment, seemingly too fragile for this world, bouncing back and craving admiration the next. His oldest grandchild was a bright kid in his senior year at Sacred Heart. As he entered the cold surf, he felt a twinge of conscience thinking about what he'd like to see Junior do with his life.

He was beginning to understand that reasonable and logical decisions could be wrong when they ignored feelings. Being trained by his grandfather to block out feelings didn't make it any easier for him to deny his Mediterranean blood. Seeing Hokmah made him think about how often he put a lid on things. Letting his heart make up his mind was not an easy thing for him to do.

A wave knocked the two Carmines off balance. He began to feel like one of the kids, as he stood up to brush the sand off.

A shudder seized Carmine. "My legs are freezing! I'm going to sit down and warm up. Come on up here when you've had enough. Angelina! It's time to come out of the water. Michael, Gabriel—give me a hand! Get the little ones up here to dry off before they get a chill. Why don't we all go back to the house, pick up Grandma, and go over to Cooke's for dinner?"

"Poppie, can I talk to you alone for a minute?"

"Sure, Junior. Let's walk down the beach. What's on your mind?"

"I'm scared to begin."

"Nothing wrong with being that Junior; I've been scared lots of times. Just remember I love you and whatever it is, I'll try to help. I was just thinking about decisions and faith. So have faith in me as I do in you and let's hear your story. Just say what you need to say."

"A few months ago, a buddy of mine from high school had some drugs..."

"Where is this going? What did—"

"That's what I was afraid of. Please let me finish."

"Sorry. I'll be quiet and try to live the sermon. Promise."

"I wanted to see what it was like. You know, experiment. I had no idea what it did to you. So, I went for it" Junior's eyes brimmed with tears. He glanced at his grandpop and saw no judgment in his face, only concern. He continued. "So, we shared a needle. He told me later that he's HIV positive. I just got my test back. I'm positive too."

The frontal vein on Carmine's high forehead bulged in sharp relief to his blood-red face. He dragged a hand through his salt-and-pepper hair.

"What's that son of a bitch's name? I'll teach him—"

"You won't be teaching him anything, Poppie. You'll be acting just like him. And I don't ever want to be like him."

CHAPTER 6

After settling in Hokmah was able to spend more time with his staff and patients. The staff was impressed by how comfortable he was working with them and even more impressed by his interactions with three difficult patients that they presented to him on rounds.

The first case was a recently admitted depressed Polish gentleman who refused to talk to anyone unless they spoke Polish, which no one on the full-time staff could do.

Hokmah walked over to where he was sitting in the conference room, and said, "*Jak sie masz*."

The patient beamed, proclaiming, "Dat's my doctor."

The staff learned later that Hokmah had asked him, "How are you?" in Polish. He felt it was no coincidence that these were the only Polish words he had ever learned from a Polish couple he had treated in the past.

Next was a woman who only spoke unintelligible gibberish. Hokmah had them record her conversations, which he played back at varying speeds, to see if she were speaking words in some bizarre pattern. The tapes verified the unintelligible nature of her mutterings.

He went up to her the following day and said, "Hubindereck muddroblest klopsdemnedered."

She responded: "Thank God, someone around here is finally making sense."

Last but not least was Willie, who believed he was Mickey Mouse and would only speak to therapists who dressed like a mouse, which most refused to do, and the few who did quickly grew tired of it.

Before their session, Hokmah put on a set of costume mouse ears he retrieved from Peaceful Acres' deep box of counseling toys, games, and props. "Willie, I'm all ears." Mind you, this was said in a pretty fair imitation of Mickey Mouse's falsetto voice—no mean feat for the doc with the sonorous pipes.

"Finally," sighed Willie, "someone I can talk to who listens and speaks my language."

Hokmah was rapidly building a caseload of the most difficult patients and the staff was very grateful. He was also wise enough to arrange for George to come for his appointment the day before Carmine's.

"Doc, I brought my dogs and jogging gear," remarked the excitable surgeon, upon arrival. "I sure hope you'll give my idea a try."

"My schedule doesn't leave time for me to change and shower. Let's just go for a walk."

"Maybe I can be your last patient of the day next time."

"I'll think about it."

The two strolled leisurely around the grounds. Hokmah wondered what Freudians would say about his casual approach to therapy. In the Freudian tradition the patient would lie on a couch, while the good doctor sat behind him or her in a chair, taking notes, never making eye contact. That was not Hokmah's style. He had learned how important people's facial expressions and listening to them were.

"Doc see that barbed wire?" asked George, pointing. "Look how the tree has grown around it. Think about doing that with an irritating problem."

"Yes, George, better to rise to the occasion than hit the ceiling. That's some good marital counseling. Let's go down to the local town cemetery for further therapy and read some headstones."

"You've got a point. I feel grateful for my health after looking at the young age some of these people died. Some of them never had a chance to experience life. I used to think every life had an unhappy ending, but these stones make me wonder. I love these epitaphs: 'He just fell up' and 'I'd marry you again.'

"See what I mean, Doc? How you get to thinking in a way that wouldn't happen in the office? Hey, I just thought of what I'm going to put on Honey and my headstone: 'Never go to bed mad. Stay up and fight and never argue with a woman when she is tired or rested.'"

"George, I appreciate your sense of humor but what does any of this have to do with your problem?"

"Do you want to hear the good news or the bad news? Never mind, let me tell you about the most interesting thing that happened first. My secretary tells me a Mr. Birsamatto wants to make an appointment to see me. I wonder, is it you-know-who. I call back. One of his associates, Michael, answers and says to call him by his first name. I ask, 'Is this *the* Carmine Birsamatto?' He tells me it is and that weekends are best for his boss and they'll drive me up and back. So, we set up a Saturday afternoon appointment and I give them directions. We'll be getting together while you're away. That should make things interesting for you when you return."

"George let's get back to the reason you're here."

"Honey thinks the two of us ought to get away together. The bad news is, I feel guilty about all my therapeutic fantasizing and don't know what to do about it. What do you think, Doc?"

"I think working on your relationship away from home, away from the kids and pets could be very helpful. Sharing some pleasant experiences can't hurt either."

"I just didn't know if it made sense; I kind of thought maybe we'd get on each other's nerves even more."

"George, that depends on your behavior and attitude. If you love your wife—and I didn't say like—and act as if you love your wife, you won't have a problem."

"I'll talk to Honey about it. Doc, thanks for being human."

"George, I've learned from my wounds too. You need to rehearse and practice until you become the person you want to be. Remember, you have a lifetime to perform."

"Good advice, Doc. I'll call to make another appointment. Maybe we can get into jogging and recycling then."

———※———

The following day Carmine appeared for his appointment. As on their first meeting, he was dressed to the nines.

"I've had some very upsetting news that derailed my concerns and gave me something new to think about," said the racketeer, without preamble. "While you were away at your meeting, I learned my grandson is HIV positive. He shared a needle with some kid at school. My reaction was to want to kill the son of a bitch. And Junior said that won't solve anything, and I'm just being like the kid I want to get even with. I felt like he hit me in the chest with a baseball bat. Nothing has ever affected me like that, and I don't know where it's coming from. I have eliminated people and problems from my life before and not been affected by people's opinions. But my grandson..."

Carmine yanked a plum-colored silk handkerchief from the pocket of his Brioni suit jacket and dabbed at his eyes. Hokmah laid a comforting palm on the elegant man's shoulder.

"Carmine, we need to look into what this is bringing up for you. While I'm away at my annual convention I'd like you to start a journal about your dreams, all your feelings good and bad, and what you need to say that has never been said before. There is no wrong way to do this. It will help you to open up your unconscious and reveal your inner truths. As they say, God speaks in dreams and images. And as Jesus says in the Gospel of Saint Thomas: 'If you bring forth what is within you, what you bring forth will save you. If you do not bring forth what is within you, what you do not bring forth will destroy you.' So have the courage to know your true self and begin your healing journey and keep notes."

"Doc, I think my grandson's words and yours have gotten through to me. I'm ready to start my journey."

"I think this is all tied together with your identity and what brought you to me. You've got a week to think and feel and then speak about it. In the meantime, don't judge your feelings, Let Junior's experience be therapy, too, and take it one day at a time. Worrying about the future never solves anything and can destroy you. Spend time listening to your grandson so he realizes what he needs to do, and you know what you need to do, and we can look at it all the next time we get together. You never know where problems will lead you."

"I think I'm beginning to get the message. It's like the labor pains of birth but it's all worthwhile when the result is a new life."

"Yes, Carmine, when you can love your fate and ask what you are to learn from the hell you are going through, you can really change your life and provide it with new meaning and direction. Just keep an open mind and live in the moment or you will ruin everyone's life. Sometimes there are spiritual flat tires which can save and redirect you. Leaving your troubles to God can do wonders too. You will find there are no coincidences. A flat tire can cause you to miss a plane that crashes and save your life. Do you feel ready to start the journey and make it a part of your daily life?"

"Yes, I'm ready to begin the journey and do more than just try."

"George tells me you and he have an appointment."

"Yes, I need some medical advice and I figure who better to trust to make the right choice than George. By the way, I hope your trip to San Francisco is safe and rewarding. I have friends there. If you need anything, call me."

"Thanks, see you when I get back."

CHAPTER 7

The long flight to San Francisco and change in time zones left Hokmah severely fatigued. Upon arriving at his hotel, he went right to his room, unpacked, and jumped into bed. When the phone rang, he reached for it, still half asleep, knocking the receiver off the nightstand.

"Good morning. It's six a.m. Currently it is forty-eight degrees. Today's forecast calls for clear skies with highs in the sixties. Have a nice day."

The American Psychiatric Association officers and committee chairmen would soon be at his door to accompany him to the president's breakfast; later in the day, he would deliver his keynote.

Hokmah threw his muscular legs over the side of the king-sized bed and stretched luxuriously. "They didn't know what they were letting themselves in for when they elected me president," he muttered aloud, rubbing the sleep from his eyes. "They just wanted someone economically, politically, and racially correct for their needs. Now it's time they deal with our profession's true needs."

He lumbered to the window of room 4304 of the Mandarin Oriental, he and his wife's favorite accommodations when they came to San Francisco. Gazing out, the view was like a landscape painting. The Golden Gate Bridge, Alcatraz, San Francisco Bay, and, at night, the lights created a jeweled city. Memories were the reason he stayed at the Mandarin, even though the APA meeting was at the Ritz-Carlton.

He was jolted back to reality by the sight of his papers and flash drive. He'd better get moving if he was going to get a run in before the meeting. He took the elevator to the lobby, dropped off his keys at the desk, and stepped into the San Francisco air. The fog rolling in across the bay created a beautiful picture, but he preferred the clouds back east to earthquakes.

The streets were filled with musicians and singers, something you rarely saw on the streets of New York or Boston. As he jogged toward Fisherman's Wharf pleasant memories flooded his mind. Not unlike his patients, he loved to let his mind produce random thoughts.

He thought about Carly Simon's "Haven't Got Time for the Pain" and Jim Croce's "Time in a Bottle," two songs whose plaintive message was the same: life's too damn short, so make the best of each and every day. He had learned from experience the key to the doors of hell can open the gates of heaven too.

As he jogged along the waterfront, he thought Alcatraz would make a nice site for a residential psychiatric center. Some patients would love to send their doctors to Alcatraz. He jogged past tourists and novelty shops as he performed his morning routine. He had learned from one of his patients "to make his own weather" and to reflect on what he was grateful for, then confess his weaknesses and pray for himself and those he cared for.

At Sansome Street he turned and jogged up to the Mandarin. Near the entrance he stopped to pick up a penny on the sidewalk reflecting the sunlight. Hokmah could never pass up a wayward penny, shiny or dull. Some of his fellow therapists thought this compulsion was a sign of psychotic behavior. He laughed remembering the time he stopped to pick up a penny while running the New York Marathon, overhearing people say, "How poor can he be?" They didn't know he had already found a quarter so now he had twenty-six cents; he knew God was sending him a sign that he would finish the twenty-six-mile marathon with flying colors.

Andy, the doorman, smiled as Hokmah slipped the penny into the pocket of his jogging shorts. The convivial fellow had been a fixture at the Mandarin for as long as he could remember. *Is he smiling because I pick up pennies?* Hokmah mused. *He probably helps more people with his smile than I do through therapy.*

"Andy," he said, "I don't know what you're smiling at, but for me pennies are my message from God. Celestial treasures that show me that I'm on my right path. Lincoln reminds me of my need to appreciate my lifetime. The mottoes 'Liberty' and 'In God We Trust' summarize my beliefs that we have the freedom to choose our way and the reason to have faith. Like peas and corn, there are different experiences, but you have to believe in everything if you are to be saved."

Andy considered this philosophy, nodding his head thoughtfully. "Reminds me of something my father used to say: a penny saved ..."—he paused for dramatic effect, knowing what Hokmah expected him to say—"is not much. Come in and I'll get you some water. You need it after your run."

Hokmah chuckled appreciatively and breezed inside.

At the front desk he picked up his keys, took the elevator up to his room, and jumped into the shower singing, "I Left My Heart in San Francisco." He was tone deaf and drove anyone unlucky enough to be in earshot of his off-key warbling crazy. His entire family was like that. They never complained because they didn't know any better. Shortly after he started dating his wife, she pointed out that fingernails dragged across a blackboard sounded sweeter than his assault on the eardrums. Now he did his singing alone in the shower or car to avoid her using it as reasonable grounds for a divorce.

He had worked hard to accept his body and keep it in shape. His cat Miracle had been his therapist. A big, black and white stray, Miracle never seemed to have a problem with her self-image when she passed a mirror, despite the kink in her tail and low-hanging belly. She probably just thinks it's me, Hokmah reasoned. So, he decided to say, "Hi, me, I love you," every time he looked at his naked body. He eventually gave his body the name Hymie and greeted it whenever he looked in the mirror. His behavior reminded him of "The Ugly Duckling" fairy tale. After suffering terrible abuse from the other farm animals, the outcast "duckling" realizes, upon gazing upon its mature reflection in a still pond that it was a swan, the most beautiful of birds, all along. If his mind and the pond were turbulent, he would never have seen his true self and beauty.

He smiled, thinking, "After creating man God didn't say it was good. Animals are complete while man is not. I just hope someday I'll be able to live up to my role model, Lassie, and fulfill my potential." He loved the idea that maybe Jesus was the only normal person who ever lived; what an awesome potential to try to live up to! And as Jesus said: "It is done unto you as you believe."

When Hokmah stepped out of the shower he greeted his reflection with, "Hymie, I love you." He lathered his bald head, shaved carefully, and trimmed his beard. He knew that shaving his head, like monks did, had a lot to do with his spiritual awakening. It helped his patients too. *After all,* he thought *if I'm wounded, I can understand them better.*

Because their training provided them with information but not the experience necessary to care for themselves or their patients, Hokmah knew many psychotherapists were treating their unresolved conflicts and not their patients' problems. They acted like they were treating mechanical objects and not minds and bodies. When people needed a referral, he suggested they find a psychiatrist who had practiced another specialty first or had experienced a significant illness and chose psychiatry for a healthy reason, like caring about people; and not just treating their diagnosis with a prescription medication, but also treating their story. He also knew that the best doctors learned from the criticism of their patients and families. They didn't make excuses and listened, so people shared their true feelings about them and with them.

It never failed to amaze him how many people discovered who they truly were and recovered when you just listened and said, "Mmmm." Yes, he'd learned from Helen Keller that deafness was darker by far than blindness.

As he started dressing his naked body, he mischievously fantasized showing up at the APA meeting in the buff. "Now, that would make an impression." He remembered once seeing a hypnotherapist undress while speaking at a conference to keep everyone's attention. Well, he wasn't that well-adjusted yet. He put on his blue banded collar denim shirt and jeans, picked out the rainbow socks his kids had given him, and slipped into his sport jacket with the lapel pins.

His guardian angel pin protected him. He just didn't tell anyone about his conversations with his angel because they might think he was psychotic. As Lily Tomlin said, "If you talk to God it is called prayer. If God talks to you it's called schizophrenia."

The attitude pin was given to him by one of his patients, who explained: "Whenever I'm feeling down my wife reaches out, twists my pin, and says, honey, you need to straighten out your attitude."

The third pin was of a set of footprints which reminded him he had choices. God could carry him; he could follow others or create his own path. As Judy said, "Being crazy is part of the cure. The first letters of Crazy, Unique, Refreshing, and Exceptional spell C-U-R-E."

Hokmah heard the voices of his colleagues in the hallway and opened the door. "Come on in, guys, be with you in a second. Just gotta put on my shoes."

One of the men glanced irritably at his watch. "Hurry it up, would you?" he said. "We've got a car waiting to take us to the Ritz."

"All right, all right, let me grab my flash drive and papers."

He wished he could get them to be more childlike. Hell, we're all multiple personalities, so why not let the kid out now and then? Kids always commented about his shaved head and beard while their parents would say, "Shhh, don't say anything."

Maybe he should suggest a masquerade party for the next meeting. What made life interesting and we, as human beings, recognizable were our external differences. Internally we are all the same color. He knew a group of doctors and nurses who dressed as clowns. He didn't trust people in uniform, doctors, or anyone else. Most of them didn't know who they were without their uniform. Like fundamentalists they needed structure and regulations to define and protect themselves, to lose their identity, and to excuse destructive behavior.

He headed for the door with the three of them following. Not one of them had said, "Good morning." They could have left out the good and just said, "Morning," but even that would be overly friendly for these stuffed shirts. They rode to the lobby in silence. He found himself grinning, thinking *I'd rather get on an elevator with three dogs. We'd rub, sniff, bark, leave a few scents for the maintenance crew, and promise to sniff each other out again.*

The staff greeted him in the lobby and got a kick out of his introducing his companions as his attorney and bodyguards. The crisp San Francisco air felt good. He climbed into the limo for the silent ride.

At the Ritz he followed his taciturn entourage to the conference room where the attendees were waiting to greet him and have breakfast. Many of them would be on a plane home tonight. Hokmah himself couldn't wait to get home, as far away as possible from the necessary evil that this conference was.

The pleasantries, as mechanical and insincere as ever, were all variations on: "Good to see you, Jon." "Thanks for all you've done." "How's the family?"

Nobody ever waited for an answer; he doubted they really cared or wanted to know, so he just shook hands or nodded. He was tired of people greeting him with "How are you?" when they really didn't want to know. He often advised these disinterested parties to just say, "You're looking very well today," which was just as insincere but at least didn't imply phony interest. He was also glad to see more women present than usual at these affairs. They, like the Jungians, were helping to keep the organization balanced and in touch with reality.

Hokmah went to the podium to introduce himself, then the newly elected officers and committee heads, and to thank the outgoing ones. The hotel staff was busily pouring coffee or juice and making sure everyone had a seat. There were too many distractions to try and say anything meaningful.

"If you're as hungry and thirsty as I am, after my morning run," his voice boomed through the microphone, "I know you won't want to delay breakfast. Let's eat and then reconvene."

Those who had not ordered a special meal lined up for the unhealthy selections at the buffet table. Hokmah selected a cheese Danish to go with his black coffee and sat down.

Sitting at Hokmah's table was a woman in her late thirties, wearing very little makeup. She returned his gaze with a sense of self-assurance. He felt an immediate desire to know her better. He read her nametag: Dr. Ingebard Bergman.

"Good morning, Dr. Bergman," he said. The table was too wide to reach across to shake her small white hand, as fine and delicate as a doll's, so he just nodded.

She smiled. "Good morning, Dr. Hokmah. Please call me Inge."

"Pleasure to meet you, Inge and call me Jon. Glad you could make it today. I'm curious: what's your specialty?"

"My committee is the one studying assisted suicide and euthanasia. I want to empower people. We seem to pay little attention to the fears people have facing death. The recent pandemic can teach us all that one's mortality can be a potent psychotherapeutic tool; death with dignity is something that truly motivates me. People have more control of their death than they understand or believe."

"I'm impressed, and I agree with you. You must be well thought of to be a committee head."

Inge didn't get an opportunity to answer as people returned from the buffet table full of small talk and griping about their special meals, which apparently weren't special enough.

Inge made him think about feminine qualities, women's strengths, and the need to give them an opportunity to express themselves. He resolved to discuss this with her after breakfast. When the increasing chatter and restlessness signaled people were done eating, Hokmah returned to the podium and tapped the mic for everyone's attention. In a few moments he addressed the now silent room.

"What I want to share with you are my feelings about the direction we, as a profession and as human beings, should be taking.

"Being a man who experienced the suicide of his parents while still a child, and felt I was a failure as a child, I am perhaps even more aware than most that no one's life is free of difficulties, and that choosing life is a personal decision. Advances in technology fill our lives yet the old song still speaks the truth about what there's just too little of and what the world needs now. Yes, love is the answer.

"One can't help but be aware of the problems facing society today relating to teenage suicide, addictions, violence, and other forms of self-destructive behavior due to the indifference and rejection children experience from parents, educators, clergy, and other caregivers. If I had not had a loving grandmother I don't know where I'd be today. She was able to accept and love me and that is why she was a grand mother who knew how to raise children. A not so easy task for those with no training and want to hide their problems or that of their children. I didn't feel a need for revenge as today's kids are doing with guns, and then comes the guilt, suicides, and more troubles.

"Information and technology do not change behaviors, but inspiration and love can. We must never forget the ailing mind is a human mind. The day every child grows up loved, wars will cease, and our planet will be healed. Our words are like clay in the hands of a sculptor; living the message of love can bring Heaven down to Earth.

"Until love is considered an integral part of our therapeutic regimen, we are not treating our patients properly. Drugs cannot replace love. Love acts through us. It sees others as individuals to love rather than to be loved by them. We are the same on both sides of the desk, so move your desks against the wall and do not create a false separation. We may fail, but we can try to help our patients become heroes, or divine children worthy of the life they have been given. I love asking my patients how they would introduce themselves to God to get them to see they are made of the divine stuff too and not defined by what they do but by being God's child.

"We are all well trained, capable therapists but it's time we become more than just good technicians. I had the pleasure of meeting Dr. Ingebard Bergman this morning. Dr. Bergman's committee is looking at assisted suicide and euthanasia. Why aren't we looking at assisted *living* and *survival*? I am not being mystical, frivolous, or sentimental when I say that I have created some new words and hope they will become the names of committees."

Hokmah turned and wrote three words on the flip chart beside him: LOVE, GOD, and MESSAGE. "The Love Committee," he explained, "will help people to live and love. The God Committee will help us to do good acts through God, and the Message Committee will help us to get the message across by touching people and their lives. Then our *wordswordswords* will become *swordswordswords*, which, like a scalpel, will not kill but cure.

"We know the effect being deprived of love, touch, and companionship has on the young. It's time parenting was a public health issue. As therapists we can become their chosen parents and reparent our patients or teach them how to reparent themselves and find self-worth and meaning. Not an easy task for an abandoned ugly duckling, but possible when one quiets one's mind. It is the still pond that allows us to reflect upon our true image and beauty, and not be hypnotized by the negative messages and words of our past.

"I speak in the hope of helping us, and our patients, become educated by our creativity and not our mortality. We are all capable of becoming strong at the broken places, but why do we need to break down to heal? We can help our patients to become supple and develop an inner strength which can resist breaking. We must get them to understand disease is a loss of health, not God and their religion punishing them. God is not the problem; people are. God is a resource.

"I hope each of you will start to implement my ideas in your lives and practices. If these committees are not created, perhaps we can establish The American Society for the Prevention of Cruelty to Humans, as a branch of the APA, to help reparent the world and eliminate cruelty and indifference.

"This afternoon I will discuss my thoughts on the subject in greater depth, but we need to seriously consider how to make love and joy components of the therapeutic process. We need to reparent our clients and the world by becoming their CD or CM: Chosen Dad or Chosen Mom. I hear so many patients talk about their parents' words eating away at them and causing their disease. One patient of mine declared I was her Bonus Dad because of my care and love for her."

As he walked away, the disapproving stares, shaking heads, and silent response didn't surprise Hokmah. He knew the wounded healers who supported him were uncomfortable displaying their feelings before their colleagues.

As the meeting broke up, he found Inge in the milling crowd. "Inge, do you have a minute?"

"Oh, hi, Jon. Quite a speech. I'm headed for Brian Weiss's workshop, but I can spare a minute."

"His work pushes my limits but it's nice to see he was invited. Minds are opening."

"Jon you judge others, so why don't you practice what you preach? Open your mind and attend his workshop. I've seen profound therapeutic changes occur following regressions. And if it works who cares about why? Don't you want to understand why you're living this life?"

"Wow, I had a weird feeling about your question. Sure, I'd like to know what God had in mind. I have no place to hide so I might as well attend. Mind if I ask about your thoughts on a case of mine?"

"Let's talk after the worksh—."

Hokmah bulldozed Inge's objection. "I'm trying to put together a therapeutic regimen involving a man who found it to be therapeutic to fantasize about killing his wife. I think as a married man I can relate to him and his feelings, but it's harder for me to understand his wife's experience. My wife's sense of humor always resolves our situations. When we laugh, troubles melt away and love returns. Perhaps you can bring balance and direction to the therapy. Your age and sex are perfect for the situation, but I don't see a wedding ring on your finger."

"I was married, and I've had my share of pain due to my husband's death from cancer, but that's not the issue and this is not the time to discuss it. I will say that I didn't become a therapist because of my problems. Again, I say: my advice is for you to open your mind. You talk about love, but how often is it included in your therapy? Presuming your patients' lives are not at risk, what if they all chose to understand, forgive, and love? Remember your little speech. All you need is love, right? How charmingly Beatle-esque. My advice is, if something isn't threatening your life, then see what love can do to cure the problem. Make love your weapon to induce change. If you are open to possibilities, the feminine will be a part of your therapy whether a woman is present or not."

"But getting the message across is not so simple."

"Therapists can be more of a problem than the people they are treating. Bring the women into the therapy sessions, help them to understand why their husbands acted the way they did and then, hopefully, find forgiveness. The men need to have some sense of what the women are feeling. Then they can progress, presuming their health and lives are no longer at risk, to healing their relationships and treating the story and not just offering a diagnosis. This is about what they want, not what you want. It is hard work for two people to create a third entity, a healthy relationship, and women need to feel free to do what makes them happy and not live a role. The same is true of men who find meaning only through work and not relationships and understanding."

"But on a practical level," Hokmah said, "what have you found to be the best ways to get him to understand what his wife has been through?"

"You might be surprised what women are capable of. When you get the men to share feelings and stop thinking, amazing things happen. Women know more about relationships and survival behaviors then men give us credit for. Read Montague's work on the practice of love and the natural superiority of women. It isn't just our hormones or how our brains are wired that makes us different. Women's lives are about relationships. Men are into doing things and their jobs. Consider what is man's best friend, a dog, and what is a girl's best friend, a diamond, and you'll realize who has better judgment."

Inge maintained a deadpan expression, which only enhanced the jest. Hokmah burst into laughter and knew why he felt so comfortable with her. She reminded him of his wife's wisdom and humor. Impulsively he grasped her small, warm, white hands in his gargantuan mitt.

"We need to get going if you want to accompany me to Weiss's workshop," she said. "He's speaking in the grand ballroom."

"Inge, would you consider coming to Connecticut and enhancing the voice of the feminine?"

"You have some nerve! I can see why they made you president. I'll let you know later."

"Come to my presentation to hear some of the details of the case. You feel like an old friend."

"Jon, I don't know why it's so important to you that I get involved. You don't know me, or my work."

"Inge, I'll look into your training and competence if that pleases you and helps to change your mind."

"There's the ballroom. Do you know Weiss? He trained at Yale."

"I don't know him, just his work. I see several empty seats in the front row. Leave it to psychiatrists to be afraid to sit in the front row. Come on Inge, I'll feel safer sitting next to you."

After they settled in, Inge said, "Jon, if I come to Connecticut, would you and your wife be willing to participate in my sessions?"

"Of course! I'm trying to resolve this problem, not complicate it. I can learn from criticism too. I can't help feeling it was no coincidence we were seated together at breakfast. My Jungian side says believe in synchronicity and the wisdom of the unconscious. Maybe we're soulmates and shared a past life."

Inge snorted. "Yeah, right. On the other hand, who knows? What makes life so intriguing are all the things we can't explain. For me, the mind and body are as mysterious and miraculous as the universe. I wish we'd spend more money exploring our inner space and less on outer space, although we probably feel safer not going within ourselves. There are psychic truths and physical truths and maybe someday we'll understand how they interact. As Jung said, maybe psyche and matter are complimentary aspects of the same thing. We need to study the science of love, God, and mind."

They were shushed by someone behind them as Dr. Brian Weiss strode to the podium.

"Pay attention, Jon," Inge whispered. "You will be fascinated and amazed and be truly educated versus feeling criticized."

CHAPTER 8

Casually dressed in khakis and a sweater vest worn over an open collared shirt with sleeves rolled up to his elbows, Weiss was the very picture of confidence and composure. He shuffled his papers, gazed briefly at the audience over the glasses perched on the edge of his nose, and began.

"I was initially skeptical, as many of you undoubtedly are, about past lives and regression therapy, but with time my experience with my patients changed my skepticism to belief. In many cases I found hypnosis and regression therapy resulted in successful outcomes where traditional psychotherapeutic techniques failed. My experience made me aware of the limitations imposed by my training, and so I began to explore these modalities.

"I am here to share my experience with you. I am not trying to change your beliefs with studies or statistics. I simply want you to experience something, through my stories, which may open your minds. You will, however, never witness or experience what you are unwilling to accept. A closed mind doesn't experience life and creation. Anyone interested in more information can read my books."

Hokmah's experience as a consultant at The Connecticut Hospice had raised questions in his mind about near death experiences and past lives that he had no answers for and no desire to pursue. He began to question the wisdom of attending the session. He turned to tell Inge that he had changed his mind but found her so engrossed in Weiss's words that he was reluctant to disturb her.

Inge nudged him. "Pay attention."

He looked up and refocused on Weiss's words.

"My words may not change anyone, but your experience can. Many of my patients' lives were changed by the insight they gained.

"When they understood their problems were rooted in the consciousness of past life experiences, they were empowered by this newfound understanding, which led to changes that traditional therapy might have taken years to achieve or never accomplish. Life, matter, and consciousness are mysteries that we need to accept and learn from. I am convinced death is not the end of consciousness and near-death experiences confirm this. Think of how many doctors' beliefs were changed by their having near-death experiences.

"During the regression you will remain in control of your thoughts and images. As the images appear, remember your being open to receiving them allows it to happen. Now, make yourself comfortable. Put your papers and books aside and begin to breathe deeply. When you feel ready look up and let your eyes close gently while you continue to breathe slowly and deeply. Let a wave of peacefulness bathe your body as you create your corner of the universe in the middle of nowhere—the place from which to begin your journey back through time and into your past. You will find yourself gradually returning to the time of your birth and the time before and the place beyond."

Hokmah glanced at Inge, who, judging by her rapturous expression, was already well on her journey. Meanwhile, Weiss continued his hypnotic dialogue.

"You can travel through space and time in any way you feel comfortable…. to a time and place that will gradually become familiar and meaningful to you. Time is not experienced by pure consciousness."

Hokmah decided not to participate but to just sit back and listen to Weiss, until Weiss looked down at him. Weiss didn't intend anything by it; he was simply surveying the participants to evaluate how quickly to proceed with his hypnotic dialogue. But Hokmah was embarrassed, thinking Weiss could see he was being a skeptic as he quickly closed his eyes.

"How fast, by what means, and what path you travel is your decision. You can journey back in time, travel back to the source of your blood stream, float back on a cloud or drift through the darkness of the birth canal until you come to the place you need to be to relive the experiences of your past. You will experience your life in reverse until you arrive at the meaningful time and place you are intended to reach. Then you will come out of the darkness into the enlightenment, as what is stored in your consciousness now becomes truly conscious and part of your awareness and experience. Your past life will be your luminary, helping you to understand what you are experiencing and why you are living your present life. You may feel that you are watching a movie about your life that you are playing a major part in."

The dialogue totally disorganized Hokmah's attempt at logical thinking. Images began to appear, as if he were watching a movie, which he tried to analyze, but it became impossible for him to continue thinking because he was no longer Jonathan Hokmah. He was a tall, white teenager sitting in a classroom with the name Danny Hoffman printed on his books. Gradually, Hokmah's mind ceased to function as he *became* Danny.

Danny rose as the bell sounded and the teacher said, "Class dismissed."

At the bottom of the stairs, Danny stopped to wait for an attractive girl to descend.

"Bev, may I walk home with you?" Hokmah was surprised by his knowledge of her name. There was still a part of his brain struggling to analyze the experience.

"Why not? We're out in public. So, I know you won't misbehave like most of your male friends do."

"Why are you always teasing and putting me down? What have I ever done to you? Can't we just be friends? You sure make things difficult."

"Danny, the abuse my mom and I experienced, before they put my dad away, is no secret. I feel the way my mother does about men. If they're like my dad, they belong in jail, too, and I want no part of them. Most guys remind me of my father and I'm tired of their rude, immature behavior. Danny, I don't have anything against you, but why should I think you're different? You're all interested in just one thing."

"When you get over what your dad did, and realize that what you think and feel is up to you and not your dad, or what he did, maybe I can help you to change your mind."

"That'll be the day."

They walked in silence until they reached Danny's house. His mother was waiting on the front porch as they came up.

"Hello, Mrs. Hoffman," said Bev.

"Hello, Bev. How's your mother?" There was as much judgment as interest in her voice.

"As well as can be expected, I guess."

Mrs. Hoffman essayed a half-smile and turned to her son. "Good news, Danny, Mr. Schultz called. He said he likes your idea about a student column for the Sunday paper."

"Wow, I'll get to my homework later. I'm going to the paper to talk to him. See you later, Mom."

"Don't be late for supper!"

As the teens returned to the sidewalk, Danny said, "Bev, did you hear that? Remember the print I did in art class where *wordswordswords* became *swordswordswords*? They can be powerful tools to heal or destroy with. How about going to Ted's party with me tonight to celebrate?"

Bev sighed heavily. "Okay, I'll give you a chance to change my mind."

That night at the party, Bev made Danny discreetly observe his male classmates' crude behavior: their off-color jokes, their clumsy and brazen attempts at copping a feel. Danny watched with varying degrees of surprise, amusement … and envy; he secretly wished he could be as bold with the opposite sex as some of these junior Lotharios.

"My mother's right," said Bev. "You're all the same, only interested in one thing. I can see it in your eyes too."

"I'm not going to argue that I'm some kinda saint or something, but we're not all the same. Hell, some of our teachers behave almost as badly. I didn't know your dad, but I know what my dad was like. You decide what you see, and how you interpret everything is because of your sick thoughts and experience."

"I said all men because that *is* my experience. Given the opportunity you all behave like animals. Actually, animals aren't as rude as teenage boys and school is less civilized than the jungle. I'll be glad when I graduate. Good night, Danny. When you guys grow up, let me know."

Bev's feelings were a natural theme for Danny's first article, "Social and Sexual Interactions of High School Students." He did a skillful job researching and composing the article, carefully avoiding any specific accusations, while citing cases of unsupervised student parties, classroom, locker room, and gym interactions, and inappropriate relationships between teachers and students. Danny intentionally wrote in a manner that would make parents question what was happening at Lincoln High and gain their attention while avoiding any direct suggestions. After all, Bev included all men in her statement, and articles were appearing regularly in the papers about sexual abuse, so Danny put it together in a way that would leave parents wondering what Danny was really saying.

Danny dropped his article off at the *Sentinel* on a day Schultz, the editor-in-chief, was away. The associate editor, after checking the word count, spelling, and grammar sent it to be typeset. Schultz, a hard-nosed veteran with no appetite for fluff or sensationalism, would have filed it in the waste basket.

When his article was printed Danny removed the page from their paper so his conservative mom wouldn't see it. The more open-minded parents, and the teachers that recognized Danny's journalistic bent, knew he was just trying to present a factual, unbiased article. However, a few outraged parents contacted the principal. Danny was told to provide the board of education with his sources and attend their next meeting with his mother, who, needless to say, was humiliated.

The principal asked several teachers to attend an emergency board meeting the next day. They were told the meetings were closed sessions. Though Danny did not mention any individual teachers in the article, one of the teacher's wives came to the meeting with him. While her husband sat stone-faced, she directed her considerable fury toward the hapless principal, with numerous icy glances at Danny and his mom.

"To think that, after thirty-five years at Lincoln, you'd even consider my husband Bill would behave improperly towards any student, let alone a female one, is ridiculous. His record is impeccable.

"You and the newspaper editor should be apologizing to the teachers, not holding meetings and insulting them by lending credence to these charges. Danny Hoffman needs an education, discipline, and perhaps a whack on the behind. If he were my son, I know what I'd do. Did his mother know what his article was about or weren't you smart enough to talk to her first? Do you know how vital it is for you to educate parents?"

"Thank you, Mrs. Mason, I—"

Before he could finish, the couple stalked out, leaving Hargrove and the board with mouths agape.

Bill Roget, Lincoln High's gym teacher, was the last to be interviewed. He had taught at Lincoln for five years and came prepared to simply deny the ridiculous accusations. The exhausted and frustrated board members were feeling a loss of self-esteem from their interactions with Danny and the Masons, which Roget could sense.

"Mr. Roget," Principal Hargrove began, "Danny Hoffman's article has disturbed a lot of parents. Obviously, we're quite concerned about the truth of these allegations. We are not here to accuse you but to obtain the facts from your perspective as Lincoln's gym teacher, since Danny Hoffman alleges certain … goings-on in your department."

Like the previous speakers, Roget stood at a microphone facing Hargrove and the board, seated at a dais. "I read the article. Danny has been through a lot, emotionally and physically including the tragic death of his dad. I don't think he meant to cause anyone any harm. I believe his article was designed to call attention to himself and to a problem that certainly exists in some high schools. I'm not necessarily saying it exists in our school. I can't speak for any other teachers, but I certainly haven't done anything improper. However, I'm glad to help clarify the situation if I can. Do you have any specific questions I can answer?"

Emboldened by Roget's politeness, the board bombarded him with questions about interactions with and between students in the gym, shower, and locker rooms.

Roget couldn't believe the nonsense he was hearing from a room full of supposedly mature adults. They were worse than teenagers with their inflated, egotistical behavior. He could understand and forgive Danny for writing such a sensational piece, but the board's behavior connected him with a lifetime of pain and grief.

"Being single, we would like to know if sexuality and gender had anything to do with your becoming a gym teacher—that is, if you are comfortable sharing," said one board member, a man in his early fifties. "We do not want you to think we are accusing you or anyone of anything; we are merely trying to gain some enlightenment and be sure the school is a safe place for the students."

He flashed an unctuous smile and reared back in his chair.

"To answer your question, I am a gym teacher because I want students to value themselves and develop self-esteem. I want them to participate fully in life and give it their best shot. Athletics is the metaphor I use to teach with and show them how their aggression can be used in healthy ways in sports. I want to be their coach and help them cope with the difficulties and challenges we all encounter. I want to help the troubled kids grow into decent human beings —something you can't seem to understand with your sanctimonious attitude."

Roget ignored the uncomfortable murmurs and seat-shifting and went on.

"I know the pain of growing up and having to hide your true identity. I am gay." The audience grew silent as Roget went on, "I thought of suicide as a teenager because I didn't want to feel different. That is why I chose to be a teacher, because I know what the kids are going through, and I wanted to help them to heal and survive and feel somebody does care and love them. Danny is one of these survivors, and his article is an example of his search for recognition and healing. You know the suicide statistics for high school students.

"I am seriously thinking about handing in my resignation because of the way I now feel about working here. I am not considering resigning because I did anything that I am not proud of as a teacher, or as a human being, but because I am tired of being associated with people like you. This is the last straw. I am so disgusted by your nonsense and your ignorant, uncaring, insensitive, and intolerant ways."

Hargrove spoke up nervously. "Mr. Roget—*Bill*—please, this isn't the proper time for—"

"This is exactly the proper time, and I'm going to have my say! I don't need to defend myself. But I can sense what some of you are thinking, because it is what I've had to deal with my entire life. I'm tired of hiding, being treated as a minority and a sinner whom God despises, and all the shit I've have put up with from the moment I revealed myself to my parents and the world. But it has never affected the quality or integrity of my work. I have no interest in the young men and women of Lincoln other than to help them grow up to be decent human beings prepared to face life's challenges. I've had my share of difficulties and I'm damned tired of the same crap day after day. Most of you don't have any idea what I'm talking about when I say I am tired of it all because you have never experienced the rejection I have from family, clergy, therapists, strangers, and people like yourselves.

"Now I know what it's like to finally feel free. Thank you all! So, take your intolerance and decide what you will do for yourselves, the school, and the community. I'm finished with you and Lincoln, living two lives, and hiding who I am. In many ways this has helped me to accept myself and have the strength to wage my revolution."

Roget turned to face Danny and his mother. "Thank you, Danny. If you hadn't written that article, I'd have never known what a bunch of hypocrites I was working for."

Neither wanting nor needing a response from Hargrove and the stunned board, Roget went to his classroom, gathered his belongings, and left on a roller coaster ride, feeling the high of self-acceptance and the low of his tragic life.

Sentinel editor Schultz, having already fielded countless complaints and inquiries from the public at large about Danny's article, was doubly incensed when word came to him of the incendiary school board meeting. He summoned Danny to lecture him and cancel his column.

"Son, you've got to straighten out this mess and the trouble it's causing. You have hurt innocent people. You need to apologize to everyone. This is not a lurid TV special—this is about people's lives."

"I'm sorry, Mr. Schultz. I didn't mean to hurt anyone. I'll do whatever you suggest."

"If you're truly sorry for what has happened and can learn from your mistakes there's hope for you. We'll publish a retraction and apology in the paper, and then see if we can turn you into a real reporter who knows how to use words to inform and inspire people."

The next day Danny went to Principal Hargrove's office to further explain everything, as Schultz had advised, from his date with Bev that had inspired the article, to his research, and ultimately his writing of the article. After conferring with the board, it was agreed Danny should formally apologize to everyone as soon as possible. At their next meeting, which he and his mother were to again attend, they would decide what disciplinary action would be taken.

Danny picked at his dinner that night. "Mom, I'm sorry and really want to make amends for the trouble I've caused."

"Danny, let's go sit in Dad's office."

Martha had left the office exactly as it was before her husband died. It was like stepping into their past. A masculine room with dark wood paneling, filled with Gilbert Hoffman's favorite books and golfing trophies and other mementoes. On his desk was a photo of the three of them, taken at Olan Mills, when Danny was ten. The room still smelt faintly of Old Spice, Gilbert's cologne.

Martha sat in her husband's rumpled leather chair while Danny perched on the edge of the desk, twirling between his fingers the owl-shaped paperweight he'd made for his dad in kindergarten. Penny, his beloved cat, leapt upon the desk and groomed herself.

"There's a lot of pain in the world, but it's not a bad thing if you give it meaning. It can be a labor pain which leads to change for the better. Most of all, son, we need to have compassion for those who are hurting, and if you can't help, be sure you don't compound the hurt. Don't make excuses: learn something. Apologize, tell everyone how sorry you are and hope they forgive you. What they do is up to them. Everything you remember, God forgets."

"Where should I start, Mom?"

"Perhaps the Masons first."

"Right! Then Coach Roget. See ya!"

Danny kissed her on the cheek, grabbed his coat off the rack in the foyer, and dashed out the front door, rehearsing what he would say.

Mr. and Mrs. Mason greeted him more cordially than he expected. He was invited to come in and sit down. After a few uncomfortable pleasantries, Danny found the courage to speak his piece.

"Mr. and Mrs. Mason, I'm so sorry. I didn't realize how much trouble my article would cause. I'll never do anything like it again. I wasn't thinking about anyone but myself. Please forgive me for the trouble I have caused."

"Danny, we have children and understand," said Mr. Mason. "The fact that you care enough to come and apologize means a lot. We forgive you and truly hope you have learned from your experience."

"I have learned a lot, and Mr. Schultz promised to teach me how to use my writing to help people. I don't want to hurt anyone ever again."

Hokmah cried Danny's tears.

"Thank you for understanding. I have to go now and apologize to Mr. Roget."

Danny arrived at the former coach's house feeling more confident. He rang the doorbell. While waiting for a response he noted a light at the back of the house and walked around the porch, glancing in the windows to see if anyone was home.

The neighbors heard him screaming and pounding on the door. Adrenaline gave him superhuman strength; he rammed his shoulder repeatedly into the door, splintering the jamb. When the door crashed open Danny knew it was too late. As he touched the cold body sprawled on the kitchen floor, he felt drained and helpless, as he had when his dad died. Nothing made sense anymore. Danny collapsed into a chair, placing his head on the table.

Hokmah continued to sob until he became aware of Inge's and Weiss's voices and their arms embracing him. He couldn't stop sobbing but began to question everything, like an analyst interpreting a dream. Did Danny's actions have anything to do with him becoming a psychiatrist? Was this why the song "Danny Boy" had always been so meaningful to him?

Weiss went back on stage while Inge stayed at his side.

"Jon, this regression may help clarify for you and the others who are attending why you are living the life you are living today," she said. "Your awareness of the past will now help you to live your true authentic life."

"Inge, I need to step outside and clear my mind. I want to thank you. And Brian too, before I leave."

At the conclusion of Weiss's workshop, the participants drifted out of the ballroom, leaving Hokmah alone with Inge and Weiss.

"Thank you, Dr. Weiss," he said, "my experience was meaningful, and though I'm still confused about past lives it's not an issue of beliefs anymore. I can no longer doubt the efficacy of regression in getting us to confront our issues."

Weiss thanked him for his participation. He and Inge left the ballroom together, leaving Hokmah alone with his thoughts. He felt unsettled and yet, in a strange way, better prepared. He picked up a cup of chamomile tea in the hotel lobby and headed for a quiet corner of the lounge, only to lose his identity as, once again, the images of his past life appeared before his eyes.

CHAPTER 9

Hokmah watched as Danny, overwhelmed with grief, burst out the door of Roget's house and staggered home to lose himself in the darkness of his dad's office. He did not move when the doorbell rang.

When Martha Hoffman opened the door, she saw Police Officer Al Plimpton standing on the threshold. His patrol car was parked in the driveway.

"Good evening, Martha. Is Danny home?"

"Something wrong, Al?"

"Sorry to say I'm here on official business. I don't know if Danny told you, but Bill Roget committed suicide."

Martha's hand flew to her mouth. "Oh my God!"

"We found a note addressed to Danny in the house and we'd like to know if it sheds any light on the situation. We're not investigating Danny's actions and we don't want to intrude into any personal relationships. We thought we'd turn the letter over to Danny and let him share any pertinent contents with us. Would you mind giving it to him, please?"

"I'll see if he's here. Please come in, Al."

After taking off his hat, Officer Plimpton followed Martha to Danny's room. Not finding him there, she went to her husband's office. Danny sat at the desk staring blankly out the window, absently stroking Penny, asleep in his lap.

"Sweetheart, Officer Plimpton is here. He just told me what happened. I'm so sorry. Coach Roget left a letter for you. Please read it before you start blaming yourself."

She held out the note. When Danny didn't respond, she turned on the desk light and began reading:

Dear Danny,

You did not cause my problems and are not responsible for my actions. Don't blame yourself. If you're willing to learn from what has happened, I can still be your teacher. My choice was a personal one that had nothing to do with you. In some ways what you did helped me.

To use a term you can identify with, my life stinks. When I told my partner what transpired at the board meeting he packed up and left. He said exposing our relationship put him at risk. That's his choice but I can't live that way anymore. I'm tired of being dishonest and not living what I teach. Try to understand, but don't feel responsible for my actions and above all don't imitate me. Pain can be your teacher and help you to define yourself. I just can't choose life when I look back at what my life has been and will be.

I have never lived an authentic life. I'm responsible for that and now have options related to my future. What I have decided to do is not about you, your article, or the school. I just don't have the courage or strength to choose life. I am too tired. I know that choosing life is what the courageous do, but I have never had the support of my family or my relationships to be able to do that. My parents' words have never stopped eating away at me and I hope this will wake them up.

Bless you, Danny. You can survive with something I never had: a mother's love and support. With her support you'll find the strength to go on. Choose life for your sake and mine. I will be watching.
Your Teacher In Life and Death,

Bill Roget

Danny continued to stare out the window. A single tear meandered down his cheek. Penny, sensing his misery, mewed plaintively. Danny realized he was at a point where he needed the courage to choose his way and path through the life he had created. Just as Roget had.

"I'll need that note, Martha—it's evidence," said Officer Plimpton. She handed it to him blindly. "I'll let myself out."

Martha went to her son, gathered him in her arms, and wept with him. Danny was expelled from school for two weeks. He wished it had been for the entire semester. When he wasn't fitfully napping, all he kept seeing was his dad's charred body and Roget's corpse. Through it all Penny remained his compassionate companion.

Danny ran into Sal when seeking to escape from his mother's well-meaning but cloying attention. Sal sat him down on his park bench and tried to share what his wounds had taught him.

"Danny, sometimes the worst things that happen can become gifts when they redirect your life. Then the curse becomes a blessing. You can do it, Danny. I see the potential and love in you. That's one of the reasons I love animals. They are great teachers about life. So, when in doubt just ask yourself: what would Lassie do?"

Despite his despair, Danny found this to be sound and amusing advice.

"Thanks, Sal. You always seem to know the right thing to say."

Martha took time off from her position as a social worker at the Menninger Clinic to be with Danny, but he was her child and not her client and refused to talk to her. She made an appointment for him to see the clinic's founder, Dr. Karl Menninger, affectionately known in the community as simply Dr. Karl. She knew that if Danny were going to share his feelings with anyone, it would be with a psychiatrist like Dr. Karl who was respected and honored for his heart and wisdom.

Hokmah remained entranced as he both lived and watched himself as Danny talking to Sal and Bev, committing suicide, leaving a bloody headstone and a lifeless body lying on his father's grave. His cup of tea crashed to the floor when Danny pulled the trigger.

"Jon, Jon! You okay? Jon, can you hear me?"

He was startled back into awareness by Inge's voice. She and Weiss stood over him in the private corner of the Ritz-Carlton lounge. Several onlookers eyed him curiously as a busboy hurried over to clean up the mess.

"Yes, yes, just startled by something I recalled. I'll be okay. Thanks."

"That's good," said Weiss. "The conference coordinator sent us to find you. You have a keynote to give"—he looked at his watch—"in about ten minutes."

"Damn, that's right. Thanks for reminding me."

"We'll see you in the ballroom, Jon," said Inge. She and Weiss took their leave.

He knew he had to get control of his thoughts before speaking, and that he needed to share what was inside him so that he could heal and, hopefully, help others to heal. He closed his eyes and breathed deeply for several minutes.

When he reached the ballroom, the audiovisual people took his flash drive and clipped the lavaliere microphone to his shirt. He assured them he had done this many times and advised them to relax, but they continued to fuss over him. He took his seat next to the podium, placed his briefcase under the table, and sat quietly watching the room fill with wounded healers, whose wounds could prepare them for love's service.

His fellow officers arrived and took their seats.

Fred Kaufman came over and asked, "Anything special you want me to say when I introduce you?"

"Keep the academic stuff to a minimum, Fred. Tell them a story about why you feel I was elected president and what this closing keynote was intended to be about."

"No problem. I don't like listening to inflated introductions and wasting time. It'll be short and sweet."

Kaufman took the podium, thanked everyone for coming, and then pointed at Hokmah.

"Two years ago, we elected this man president to help guide our profession through some tough times. You don't need me to tell you the problems we face practicing medicine today. I believe Jon has done an excellent job."

He paused until the smattering of applause had subsided. Hokmah knew his controversial remarks earlier in the day had raised eyebrows.

"Today's keynote was originally designed to update all of you on our progress and new sense of direction. However, Jon asked us to grant him extra time and freedom. And we did, even though we had no idea what he intended to share. We support him in his quest and want to share in his journey. He may feel he was elected president for symbolic reasons, rather than for his abilities, but I know differently. I know the man who is Jonathan Hokmah.

"As many of you know, Jon is a terrible singer." Laughter and murmurs of acknowledgment rippled through the audience. "The word quest just reminded me of hearing him sing 'The Impossible Dream' once … and once is enough." More laughter, with the hardiest coming from Hokmah himself. "So, without further delay let me introduce Dr. Jonathan Hokmah, to present our closing keynote."

Hokmah arose to more applause than expected; he guessed he had more supporters than he thought. He felt as if he was looking at them through Danny's eyes, and that empowered him.

"Thank you, Fred, for that flattering introduction. Your check's in the mail."

Appreciative laughter followed. "Fred was right. This talk is neither about the APA nor my ego but rather about my pain and growth. I asked for time so that I could share the events which have been transformative in my life and practice; some of which happened many years ago and some just today. I wish they were a part of our training too.

"If you believe in synchronicity, and that there are no coincidences, you will be intrigued. This morning Dr. Ingebard Bergman sat at my table and convinced me to attend Brian Weiss's regression workshop. Despite my disbelief I had a transformative experience and now have no doubt we are impregnated by the consciousness of past and present lives. I firmly believe that life is a school from which we are to learn and hopefully come to understand why the world and our lives have so many difficulties. We can all be enlightened by what we experience. A perfect world is not creation. We are all here to live and learn.

"If we do not bring forth what is within us, it can destroy us. We are all wounded but only those who are brave enough to reveal their wounds and learn from them become true therapists. Walk into your office with a cane or bandage over your eye and listen to what patients share for the first time because they see you are wounded too. Wounded healers are the only true healers because they are not tourists and they understand our wounds have meaning. They are, in a sense, like the labor pains of self-birthing and the new self makes all the pain worthwhile. Wounded healers know what is being lived, experienced, and felt by their patients and families—and that in love's service— only the wounded soldier can serve.

"We need to once again ask the question: whom does the Grail serve? Where is the real treasure and who is the real hero? It is no longer appropriate to simply attack a disease with a sword. We need to use the harp, as well, just as Tristan did. We need a harp and a sword and to bring the feminine back into psychiatry and medicine to work with the masculine, so we are not just treating a diagnosis but caring for people. We must suffer consciously and let love act through us. We must see others as individuals to be loved and not just as a source of love. The ailing mind is a human mind, and the soul must be healed and not just treated. In other words, we must learn to not just do something but to be something to our patients. And prescribe what their soul needs to heal their spirit and body.

"Why are we all wounded and troubled? Why do physicians commit suicide more frequently than their patients? Because a perfect world would be a meaningless magic trick, with a high unemployment rate and very short evening news. We are here to show compassion to the wounded and help them to find love so they can treasure the experience of life, as difficult as it may be.

"I went through hell as a child, feeling like an unlovable failure, after my parents committed suicide. I don't blame them or myself any longer. I ask what I can learn from them. How I can love my fate and learn from my hell so that I no longer think of their actions as evil, but rather as something which can motivate me to be creative and not feel like a failure? My parents' actions helped me to understand the experience of those who loved me in my past life, and how to survive despite the pain of loss. Something, I would add, I was incapable of handling in my past life.

"And though the source of life is divine, loving, intelligent conscious energy, living is about matter becoming conscious and, therefore, filled with difficulties. So, let us not forget, the flame of a candle reaches towards heaven and spirit, but the candle's wick remains in the physical world. And though the seeds come from above, we must all put down roots in the earth to sustain life and bring heaven to earth by our actions. The eternal principle which must govern man is love, and we must show it through our essence.

"Psychiatry is still learning about psyche and soma. Freud, Adler, Jung, and others should have our admiration. We see the pharmaceutical ads in every medical journal. None tell you to talk to patients or explore their dreams and symbols. They tell you to just give them a pill. We are writing prescriptions to treat a diagnosis while ignoring the patient. As Jung said, the diagnosis may help the doctor, but it doesn't help the patient. We need to explore inner space and its meaning for every patient. For it is within each person that there lives a story and the truth only they can know and need help with. It is the story which reveals our patients' experience and suffering. Only after we listen to and *know* the story does our therapy begin to operate. Life is an instrument we must help our patients learn to play.

"When you study patients who do well you discover they have many similar traits and behaviors. This is what we need to teach and not respond with 'here's a pill.' Pharmaceutical companies are interested in income more than patient outcome. Every human being is unique. We must help each one find a sense of meaning in this crazy experience we call life, and to understand that peace comes when we relinquish our desires, not when we achieve them. When we give what we want to receive, it comes back to us.

"I think our fears have led us into outer space rather than inner space. Remember Columbus, who, by using subjective assumptions, a false hypothesis, and a route abandoned by modern navigation, nevertheless discovered America. Our myths, fantasies, dreams, and symbols are real. Whatever we see or discover, we do through our own eyes. And so, science cannot come from one man. I need you to open your minds and help me to redirect psychiatry so Carl Jung can rest in peace … and I can sleep in peace."

Kaufman slipped a note onto the podium, hoping to make his friend aware of the stunned audience's reaction to his emotional and seemingly personal and at times irrational presentation, but Hokmah ignored the note and the fact that some of his audience was already leaving as he continued.

"We are in pain because we are conscious. Animals, children, and the very aged don't have the problems of knowing that we have, because they have not yet become conscious or are living in their unconscious. Within each living thing is the consciousness of those who have preceded them, and until we connect with what is within us, we cannot live our authentic lives. Instead, our intellect and ego take over and destroy our authenticity.

"As Jung said, 'Every problem, therefore, brings the possibility of a widening of consciousness, but also the necessity of saying goodbye to childlike unconsciousness and trust in nature.' So, let us help people grow and learn and make a difference. To quote Jung again: 'The personalities of the doctor and patient have often more to do with the outcome of the treatment than what the doctor says or thinks—although we must not undervalue this latter factor as a disturbing or healing one.'

"I don't want anyone to strive to be normal or try to be perfect. I want them to be successful at becoming complete and living fully. Man is most human when he is joyful. So, let us help people to find their chocolate ice cream and to live their joy. Material wealth may talk but chocolate sings. Happiness, personal growth, and knowing that what you have is enough are what make someone a success.

"Let us live what we preach and ask ourselves what God asked Adam: 'Where are you?' If you are not happy as a therapist, then get therapy or quit and live the life you choose for healthy reasons, and not the unhealthy ones imposed upon you that ruin our lives and our patients' lives. Do not accept that there is no one to save because the world is in a grave. Life's unhappy ending doesn't have to follow a happy life. Something greater than we can sense, something beyond human experience—an infinite Thinker, thinking mathematically, as physicist Sir James Jeans termed it—exists, and is our avenue to healing. Remember everyone has the potential to grow and heal. As New Thought luminary Ernest Holmes said, 'What if Jesus was the only normal person who ever lived?' Jesus was an excellent therapist. His words reveal many truths about life."

Kaufman rose and took the podium microphone. "Our time is up. Jon, thank you for speaking from your heart."

Undeterred, Hokmah continued to address the audience through his lavaliere microphone.

"Sorry if I ran over, Fred. I just wanted to share that the attitude of the psychotherapist is infinitely more important than the theories and methods of psychotherapy. We are the same on both sides of the desk, just as we are at both ends of the rifle. Better yet, put your desk against the wall and have no separation. I will close with the words of Jung, and perhaps the remainder of what I had planned to say can be presented at a future meeting.

"'Both the doctor and the patient need to display their emotions. I practice as Jung did. Listen to his words: 'I reject the idea of putting the patient upon a sofa and sitting behind him. I put my patients in front of me and I talk to them as one natural human being to another, and I expose myself completely and react with no restriction.' The patient's problem is precisely to learn to live his own life, and you don't help him when you meddle with it.

"I want us to help the patient to see that the guarantee of his happiness, or his life, is not in things outside himself. The treasure lies within us and not in placing our consciousness in an object. Thank you."

Most of the audience had begun walking out, muttering, and shaking their heads, before he finished speaking. A small group, however, including Inge and Fred, approached Jon with admiration and gratitude as he was escorted through the lobby to the waiting limo. They let him know they admired his desire to humanize medical care and focus on the people they were caring for and not just the disease they were treating.

When the limo pulled up at the Mandarin, Andy, the doorman, greeted him and Plinio, the bellman, insisted on carrying his attaché case and other items to the elevator.

"How'd the meeting go, Doc?"

"Personally and, I hope, professionally enlightening. The problem is that we all see in others what dwells within us. Therefore, what is heard or seen is always interpreted personally.

Plinio's question caused him to reflect upon the few who had earnestly requested him to return and share his experience more fully—a complete surprise which gave him hope that a small group could still make a difference.

Since he was taking the red eye back to New York he packed, ordered a meal, stretched out on the bed, and dozed fitfully until awakened by a knock on the door. He let the bellboy in, signed the check, sat down to eat, and turned on the TV.

A movie called *The Dream Team* was on HBO. Assuming it was a sports film, Hokmah reached for the remote to change the channel but paused when wild-eyed Christopher Lloyd, who's convinced himself he's a sanitarium psychiatrist, appeared. He laughed as Lloyd and his fellow patients managed to get in and out of trouble and made a mental note to show the movie at one of the patient-therapist workshops. No coincidence. Maybe being normal was just an act.

He finished his sandwich laden with veggies and started to repack his attaché case. A note with a sketch of his family and their pets and "XOX I Love You Sweetheart XOX" fell out. He smiled, recalling his wife's habit of sneaking notes into his things. The symbolic kisses and hugs felt good. God knows how long it had been in there. He tucked it into his shirt pocket right next to his heart. It created feelings he hadn't experienced for some time. He laughed remembering another note of hers which simply said, "Hold on." It had helped him to hold on and get through a tough experience. When he got home and thanked her for being so intuitive, she told him that she wrote it because she put a sandwich with a lot of veggies in his bag for him and just wanted him to hold on. It made him realize how his wife's sense of humor was powerful therapy and that when they laughed together problems evaporated.

Next, he called his office answering machine, left a tip for the housekeeper, and headed out the door. He said goodbye to the staff while Andy carried his luggage to the curb and whistled for a cab. Hokmah tipped him and climbed into the cab.

"Going to the airport. United," he told the cabbie.

"Yes, sir. Headed home?"

"Yes. I love this city, but it'll feel good to get into my own bed again."

Hokmah leaned back as the cab entered the highway. There was little traffic and the ride to San Francisco International Airport went quickly. He checked in at United's first-class ticket counter and headed for his departure gate. He spied Inge walking ahead of him and hurried to catch up to her.

"Inge, wait a minute!"

She turned, smiled, and waited.

"When does your plane leave?" Hokmah asked her, a little breathlessly. "Do you have time for a cup of coffee? My treat."

"Love a decaf latte. I'm on the United flight to JFK at eleven. I have a meeting in New York tomorrow morning."

"I'm on the same flight. What happened to your committee meeting?"

"We held it last evening to save everyone a day. Assisted suicide has become an emotional topic. Between Kevorkian, euthanasia, and cult suicides, we had quite a session."

They ordered coffee at a café in the international food court and sat sipping it and making small talk until the plane started boarding.

"Where are you seated, Inge?"

She referred to her boarding pass. "Let's see ... 2A. How about you?"

"I'll be right back."

Inge was surprised to see Jon run back to the boarding gate and talk to the attendant. When he returned, he was smiling broadly.

"Good news, Inge. I was able to change seats and get 2B so we can dialogue some more."

"Here comes trouble. Let's make a deal. You let me sleep and I'll come to Connecticut. You get it organized and I'll fit it into my schedule."

"Why the sudden enthusiasm?"

"Because I need my rest. No, seriously, I think what you're doing is meaningful, even if you are a little off the wall. And I'd like to help."

"I appreciate that, Inge."

At that moment they heard the boarding announcement. When they got settled into their seats, they picked up the conversation where they'd left off.

"Just so you know where I'm coming from," said Inge, "my husband David died three years ago after complications from a bone marrow transplant for leukemia. We were very much in love; it wasn't an easy or pleasant experience, to put it mildly. I was an internist at the time. His death led me to see things differently. I realized how little help I received as the wife of a dying man. I think it was harder for my colleagues because I was a doctor. I wasn't much better with my patients but at least I was aware of their pain after David's death. I started support groups for grieving families and decided to go back for more training. I took my psychiatry residency at Beth Israel. I'm on the staff there now.

"Obviously, my life influences the way I practice. For me, the Big C stands for Compassion; what is evil isn't the illness, but rather failing to respond with compassion to the person with the illness. Embracing that philosophy, along with some of the incredible mystical experiences after his death, changed me and my beliefs. I think you can understand where I'm coming from now."

"You bet I can, Inge. The wise learn from their troubles. I realized after the regression that a big part of my choosing to rescue people and animals is not about this life's experiences, but about my past life and trying to make up for the damage I did to other people and their lives.

"Jon, I understand all that but convincing a woman whose husband fantasized killing her that she can still make her marriage work won't be easy. But then again, understanding, forgiveness, and a little love can do amazing things. Even Joseph Campbell called marriage an ordeal because it's not about our personal desires but about two people creating a relationship."

"I have learned from my childhood that forgiving the unforgivable and loving the unlovable can do wonders. Let's see what we can do."

"Yeah, I heard a fellow say that if you want to be a rebel, be kind. Jon it's what I call a love warrior. Gandhi was a great example."

Hokmah was about to mention watching *The Dream Team* when the flight attendant began the safety announcements. By the time she finished Inge had unfolded a blanket, inserted ear plugs, covered her eyes, and curled up against the window. He could see she was a seasoned traveler.

Hokmah reached into his pocket to get his eye shade and felt Judy's note again. He nudged Inge to show her his wife's note and say he could understand her painful loss better now because of how important he and his wife's relationship was to him. Inge was either asleep or was pretending to be. He didn't disturb her further.

Hokmah held onto his security blanket, wondering when Judy had put it in his case. He knew there were answers to their problems and that if they worked together, healing would be the result. He wondered if she would sit in on their sessions, too, and what he should share about his regression with his family and his patients.

CHAPTER 10

With Hokmah away, George had time to stretch out in the sun in his backyard patio. Though he felt uncomfortable doing it, he was learning that being still was an activity, just as jogging was. The problem was, he found it harder to quiet his mind than rest his body. He couldn't end the turbulence and create a still pond because as soon as he stopped doing something to distract himself, and tried to reflect upon his life and meditate, the voices began.

"Why does Carmine want to see me? Is it to teach me a lesson? Does he really need medical advice? Is his request legit or for criminal and illegal purposes? Relax—you'll learn soon enough what is expected of you."

Honey's voice brought him back to reality. "George, remember the sunscreen!" she yelled from the house. "Oh, and George, what was the name of the Mafia guy you have an appointment with? Was it Birsamatto? I was watching the news this morning and he was being questioned about some guy named Bugsy Benjamin disappearing."

"Yeah, that's the guy. I don't know what he wants of me and whether it's about my embarrassing him at the psychiatrist or family health issues or healthcare insurance advice. I can't be comfortable about it until I know for sure that it's all personal and not criminal. If I don't return from my appointment tomorrow, call the police and FBI."

"George, you've got to be kidding. If you're really worried, then don't go."

George's head was spinning, as his fantasies played out in his mind.

"I'm going to call him right now and try to find out."

He reached for his smartphone on the wrought iron table alongside the chaise longue on which he reclined. Carmine's secretary answered the call.

"Hello, this is George Dingfelder. I'd like to confirm the time of my appointment and to get some sense of how I should prepare for Mr. Birsamatto."

"Mr. Birsamatto is just interested in medical advice relating to his wife and a startup health care facility," said the secretary matter-of-factly. "My advice to you, Mr. Dingfelder, is to simply be yourself. Mr. Birsamatto does not suffer phonies gladly."

Click.

Without Hokmah to talk to, George's fantasies became his reality again. "We could exchange favors. That could really be good for business. Imagine me George Dingfelder, the Mafia medical man! A partnership would resolve all my fantasies. No need to know about sabotaged fuel lines, brakes, or seat belts. Wow."

If the appointment had not been the following day George's head would have exploded. He spent the morning standing at the picture window in the great room, his head and heart pounding, until the limo pulled up.

George opened his front door for Michael and Gabriel and stood waiting with his arms raised.

Michael and Gabriel exchanged puzzled glances.

"What are you doing?" Michael asked.

"Aren't you going to frisk me or use a metal detector?"

The man-mountains burst out laughing. "You've been watching too much TV," said Gabriel. "Mr. Birsamatto is a businessman. People tend to be suspicious of him because of the publicity he gets, but you'll find he's a considerate and sensitive man. Just be straight with him and see for yourself. Let's not get off on the wrong foot by being late."

"I'm ready. I've got everything I need."

Despite the fact Michael and Gabriel looked like they could go toe to toe with The Rock, they seemed like perfect gentlemen. They answered George's questions while not asking anything of him, so it was easy to relax in their presence.

The Birsamatto estate was classic *Godfather* stuff: electric gate, long driveway, and majestic Tudor-style house with tennis court and pool. The house was as impressive inside as out. After a brief tour, including the gourmet kitchen and indoor gym, and the den, into which George's entire house could have easily fit with room to spare. He was admiring the paintings—works by old masters, impressionists, and contemporary artists—when Carmine entered the room, dressed in a white polo shirt and matching shorts and twirling a tennis racquet in his right hand. George noticed the ostentatious signet ring on his pinky and the fine sheen of perspiration on his brow and muscular, tanned legs. He had obviously just come from the tennis court.

"You look younger and slimmer every time I see you, Mr. Birsamatto."

"Cut the obsequious crap, George. Let's get down to brass tacks. Personal recommendations have led me to believe you focus on meeting all your patient's needs."

"Why, yes. My goal is to provide the best care with the most reasonable personal costs. I don't confuse people and cover up the craziness of medical care costs by making it all sound like a dream world, with hospital costs leaving you with longer terms of payment than you ever expected. I'll give you straight talk and options you can understand and let you decide what meets your needs."

"Your philosophy is very similar to mine and useful in my business. I give people options and we work out the best solutions. Of course, if you put the dollar bill first what seems best to you may not be what's best for the patient.

I know how I resolve conflict. What do you do with your patients, George? I hope you don't mind my calling you George. Michael, please take my racquet. Sit down. Make yourself comfortable."

George sat gingerly in a grand Christopher Guy art deco-style armchair that all but swallowed him whole. Carmine sat in a matching chair, clearly unconcerned about getting sweat on the fine furniture.

"Mr. Birsamatto, if it helps us do business and feel comfortable with one another, you can call me whatever you like."

"Thank you. And feel free to call me Carmine. Can I get you a cappuccino? A cannoli maybe?"

"No, thank you … Carmine."

Carmine flicked his wrist at Michael and Gabriel, their signal to depart. "Don't look so nervous, George," he remarked. "Smoke 'em if you got 'em."

"I, uh, don't smoke."

"I figured as much." Carmine reached into the humidor on the end table beside him and plucked out a cigar. "Four hundred fifty bucks apiece, but worth every puff," he said, lighting up, to George's surprise, with a simple matchbook. "You know, George, you amuse me. I don't meet a lot of guys like you in my profession. You're quirky; I like that. So, tell me more about how you envision our business relationship."

"Well, Carmine, I don't work for an insurance company or hospital, I work for you. If you're happy, I'm happy, and I know I'll benefit from referrals in the future. My reward is the feeling of satisfaction I get from fulfilling a patient's needs."

"Sounds good to me."

George felt a little more comfortable. He crossed his legs and drummed his fingers on his bony knee. "Tell me, Carmine, what are you looking for? I prefer to look over a person's total health picture and then outline what I believe is best. There are many payment options to choose from."

"I appreciate your desire to be thorough, George, but finances aren't an issue. I have plenty of financial advisors. I want to work out the best surgery indicated for a problem my wife has, and I need your help with a large-scale health care coverage plan for members of an HMO I have an interest in."

"It's a crazy business when you purchase life insurance for death and health insurance for sickness."

"George, save the philosophy for another client. My wife is in excellent health. She's one of those exercise nuts. You saw our gym; she's always trying to get me to work out, but I can't get into that repetitive exercise—I prefer competitive sports, like tennis and golf, where I can enjoy fresh air. The problem is, she just had a mammogram that showed a suspicious spot."

"So, your wife's an exercise enthusiast, eh? Me, I love to run. Your wife is right: exercise helps increase survival statistics for all types of health problems."

George could see by Carmine's stony expression that he did not want advice.

"Sorry, I'll need to know your wife's medical history, then schedule an exam and some tests based upon her exam and mammogram and what type of surgery she wants. Shall I meet with her too?"

"No need. I'll let her know about the preliminary stuff. I'll want all the facts before we make a decision. As an aside, I have also been advised by my tax attorney to take out a three-million-dollar life insurance policy to cover estate taxes and protect my family."

"Did your attorney discuss this with you? If the policy is owned by a trust it is not considered part of her estate or yours."

"George, stick to medical advice. My attorney and accountant keep me informed about other options. I can see you're thorough. Last but not least, everything we discuss is to remain private. Do you understand, and can you live up to that? If not, our relationship is over."

"No problem. No one else need know about our interactions. If you make available your wife's medical information, I'll get back to you with the best treatment options."

"Fair enough, George."

Carmine bounded out of his chair like a man half his age. Feeling rather foolish, George clambered out of his like a turtle stuck in the mud and shook his host's proffered hand. Carmine pressed a button on the intercom system to summon Michael and Gabriel. The men appeared like magic and took their places on either side of the den's oval entryway, looking like Greek statues.

George could sense an icy shift in Carmine's demeanor. George knew he had put his foot in his mouth by offering unwanted insurance advice. He declined Carmine's second, much more perfunctory offer for refreshments. Michael went to pull the limo around for George's trip back to Danbury.

Carmine led the way to the door. "George, I hope we will be able to work things out. I don't need insurance advice. I need you to get the job done and keep your mind clear. I am more than who you think I am. Here's the limo. The boys will see you safely home. If you need anything, let them know."

"Thanks for clarifying things. I'll call you as soon as I have all the medical information and test results then we can all discuss the option you prefer."

"Call when you're ready. This is not a competitive situation. I'm relying on your ability and integrity. Once we have this worked out, we can go into the new public health care coverage plans I mentioned."

George walked down the steps feeling Carmine's gaze on his back. He didn't turn around, knowing you didn't challenge the leader of the pack by looking into his eyes. His dogs had taught him there were times when submissive behavior was survival behavior. He climbed into the limo.

"I'm closing the partition so I can take a nap."

"No problem, Mr. Dingfelder," said Gabriel, who was riding shotgun while Michael drove. "We'll let you know when we get to your place."

George closed the partition, leaned back, and put his feet up. He was in no shape to nap. He just needed some privacy to try and quiet his exhausted, scared, excited, and confused thinking about his options. Thinking was always easier than feeling.

"God damn it! I bet I know what he's thinking but for him it's no fantasy. If I can look him in the eye and share what I think is going on, we might both be beneficiaries with our finances in great shape and our futures filled with options. But do I really want to go from fantasy to reality?"

He'd get the facts together quickly to impress Carmine and then decide what to do. George knew that Carmine didn't have a problem he couldn't solve. The more he fantasized about it, the more troubling and appealing it became. Maybe there were benefits to their working together that would eliminate the risk. He felt like he was writing a script for a movie again and losing touch with reality.

What could he offer Carmine to get him to participate in his fantasies and make them possibilities—and not get himself killed in the process? What power did he have and was he willing to take the risk? If they eliminated him, his troubles were over. It might not be the preferred solution, but it was an option.

He continued to put it all together on the ride home. He was writing the script for his biggest case ever by creating a plan that would assure him of a real life if he had the guts and brains to carry it out. His first step was to get the information together and impress Carmine. He was so involved in his thoughts that Michael's touch startled him.

"Mr. D, you're home."

"Thanks, Michael. Smooth ride. I had a nice rest."

Michael held the door open for him while Gabriel looked up and down the street, as if anticipating a drive-by shooting. George said his goodbyes, walked up the steps, entered the house, and went directly to his office. Honey's head appeared in the doorway.

"Hi, dear. Everything okay? You look tired. Would you like a sandwich? Some cocoa? Maybe you should take a nap."

"Honey, what I need is peace and quiet. I just had a very intense meeting. I need time to work things out. I'll be out in a little while."

"I thought we were going out for Chinese food and a movie? I arranged for a sitter."

"We'll talk later. I need to get my thoughts together. Find something to do. Go turn some lights off. I need time to think. Please!" He scrambled to his feet and slammed the door in her face.

Honey got the message. She leaned against the closed door, wondering about George, as his mind went back to fantasizing about his options with no sign of emotion. He had learned enough about cars from his brother to know how someone could rig up a car to kill an adversary and make it look like an accident. It was just like a surgeon deciding which procedure was the correct one to perform to cure the problem. A cut in the power steering belt, a kink in the brake line, and a defective seat belt would do it. He visualized the difficulty steering, stepping on the brakes, feeling the resistance created by the kink in the line, and if the accelerator pedal stuck … KA-BOOM! Goodbye, cruel world.

Carmine presented him with a new script, but his personal fears temporarily numbed him. He knew he needed help when he imagined Carmine was thinking about using surgical complications to eliminate his wife … and then Carmine returning the favor by helping George off Honey.

Like an irrational, caged dog given an electric shock—that was his first marriage. The dog moves over. You shock the other side of the cage—that was his second marriage. The dog still has hope as long as it can retreat to a safe side of the cage. You shock the entire cage. With no safe haven to retreat to all hope is lost. Open the cage and the dog doesn't move.

George knew he was being irrational, but his fantasizing made him feel empowered and creative. He was no longer a submissive dog. He had fantasized smashing the cage but how much more efficient it would be if professionals carried out the job. What if the accident didn't work or the police were suspicious? It seemed obvious it would be a cleaner job if people "in the business," so to speak, carried it out. He was good at surgery. They were good at what they did.

Fantasies were therapeutic but he knew he needed to work out a deal because, though he was good at fantasies, he could never hurt anyone. He felt his love for Honey even when he didn't like his life.

If I could somehow stop fantasizing and just get Carmine to admit he plans to eliminate his wife, maybe he'll open up if I share my problems and offer a solution, George mused. Then by alerting the police no one would be hurt, and I could stop fantasizing and write about it and make money on a book or movie about the whole story. Instead of hurting anyone I could turn it all into a gift. Man, what publisher or movie company wouldn't jump at a story about Carmine's life! I'll make him an offer he can't refuse and have the information first thing Monday morning to impress him. I'll tell Honey I'm under a lot of pressure, so she won't ask me too many questions.

The idea is a little scary, but if I get him to think we both want to eliminate our wives I could *save* their lives by conspiring with him and letting the authorities in on it all. I don't know what will evolve or what to tell Honey, but I'll just take it one day at a time. If I were my own psychiatrist I would say, "You're nuts." A bit of humor helped him to relax, breathe again, and return to reality.

CHAPTER 11

U pon landing in New York, Inge headed off to grab a cab while Hokmah hopped on the escalator to the baggage area to meet his limo driver. Don saw him and waved. The drive back to Connecticut gave him time to reflect on how the regression was going to affect his life and practice. Should he give all his patients, including George and Carmine, the option? Perhaps he should introduce group sessions with the wives as part of the group so they could all face their issues with a woman therapist present.

With everyone home again, getting things done—whether medical, financial, or criminal—became an issue for them all.

On Monday George called Carmine's office. "Please tell Mr. Birsamatto that I have the information ready for him."

The curt secretary informed him: "He is out of town on business this week."

"Have someone call me who can make the appointment and tell Mr. Birsamatto I'm ready to meet with him at any time."

"I'll give him the message."

Click.

The delay created a problem: it gave George time to think, which was always a double-edged sword. He knew he could eliminate his present situation and start a new life but why should he have to start over? He needed a sign, a green light, to let him know if he was on the right path. He opened the morning paper to look up his horoscope and absentmindedly turned on the TV. When the phone rang, he hit mute.

"Hello, Mr. Dingfelder?"

"Yes, who's this?"

"It's Michael, Mr. B's associate. The office told us you called, and he would like to complete the arrangements for his wife's surgery as soon as possible. I'm calling to set up an appointment."

"Fine, I can come over whenever he's free."

As they spoke George glanced at the TV. There was Carmine coming out of a hotel in Atlantic City. It had to be an act of God, his green light. This was no coincidence. The message was clear. He didn't need to read his horoscope or consult a fortune teller.

"Michael, I see on TV that Mr. B's in Atlantic City."

"That's why I'm calling. Could you find the time to come down here if we send a limo for you?"

"No problem. Tell me the time and place far enough in advance and I'll rearrange my patient schedule. Oh, and Michael—please ask Mr. B if I could have a few minutes to discuss a personal issue after we work out the medical decisions related to his wife."

"Will do. He's used to people wanting to consult with him. The limo will be at your place at nine Friday morning; that should give you enough time to make plans. If there are any problems call the Fairfield number and they'll get a message to us."

On Friday George was up and waiting at the crack of dawn. Honey arose at 8:45 and found him staring out the picture window. She knew something unusual was happening.

"George, do you need help with anything? I need to know what's going on."

"You have trouble running the house so how do you expect to help me? And don't bring your brother into this. He may be my surgical partner but—"

"When are you seeing your therapist again?"

"Next week. Why?"

She was used to his obsessive nature, but this was not the man she married.

"I'm worried about you and our marriage. I do love you, but our ability to listen to each other and communicate just isn't working anymore. That is not a relationship."

"I apologize. I'm trying to change and calm down, but things keep happening."

Honey went up to the bedroom to phone her brother. "Doug, why does he have to go to Atlantic City?"

"What are you concerned about? This is just a surgical consultation with someone who wants confidentiality and privacy. He can't talk about it. It isn't another woman; I know that much. I think he's just got a lot on his mind. Give him some time. Things will straighten out. They always have. Why don't you talk to Eunice? Ask her to join you. That'll give George some space from both you and his ex-wife."

Honey planned to call Eunice as soon as George was out of the house. Maybe she knew something or heard something on one of George's visits. Her thoughts were interrupted by George telling her the limo had arrived. She gave him a hug and goodbye kiss to which he showed little response.

"George, maybe we should think about taking a little a vacation. We could get away for a few days, just the two of us. The kids can stay at my brother's. What do you think? We haven't had a vacation in years."

"We'll talk when I get home. I'll give you a call later to let you know what time to expect me."

"George, I'm frightened. I lost one husband and I don't want to lose another. Why can't you tell me what's going on? Is it your health? A business problem? Are you just tired of me? What? I know you well enough to see the change and I don't like having our marriage fall apart. I'll go for therapy with you. We have too much at stake, here George. George?" The limo horn drowned out her words. George nodded goodbye, impressed by her sincerity. The front door slammed shut with a note of finality.

Carmine offered the quickest and simplest way to solve everything. George had needs, too, and was tired of trying to figure things out and having to be strong. Gabriel held the limo door open for him. Climbing in, he nodded to Michael in the driver's seat and settled himself, reviewing what he planned to say. Closing the partition and his eyes, he remembered the daily affirmation on his calendar: Better to rise to the occasion than hit the ceiling.

He was awakened by the change in the limo's speed and the curve of the highway exit. He sat up, straightened himself out and was ready when they arrived at the hotel. Gabriel escorted him to the lobby while Michael parked the limo.

"Mr. D, Mr. Birsamatto is at a luncheon meeting," Gabriel informed him. "He thought you might be hungry after your long drive. I'll take you to his suite and get you something to eat. He said he has time to spend a few minutes on your personal problem."

"Sounds good. Lead the way." They walked to the elevator. Gabriel inserted the key card for the concierge level, which Carmine's group occupied.

"This is a combined business and pleasure trip," Gabriel remarked. "The boss often brings family and business associates with him when he goes places. Sometimes he even brings his grandchildren, especially if the meeting is in Orlando. He loves those kids. They help him put up with his business problems."

They went on for a few minutes about Mr. B's love for his grandchildren and how different he was when they were around.

Gabriel escorted George into a room with a buffet table laden with a smorgasbord of sumptuous cuisine.

"Go ahead, Mr. D, get a plate and help yourself. I'll let the boss know when you're ready."

George's mouth watered at the elaborate spread. Though his stomach made grumbles of protest, he heaped his plate with baked ziti with sausage, oyster pie, brandied figs, and two Cornish hens glazed in molasses. He had no idea what effect the next hour would have on his life but felt ready to take the risk. As he sat down to eat it all felt unreal. Was he dreaming? He realized he was taking a step with which his conscience was still struggling. He was really feeling confused about his life and decisions, and yet he felt the fantasizing empowered him and helped him get through the day. He just knew inside himself that he couldn't hurt anyone. An all-important edict from the Hippocratic Oath kept tumbling through his mind: First do no harm.

How can I talk about eliminating a woman who worries about whether I have sunscreen on? She really loves me. She drives me crazy, but she really cares. Face it, you can't be a part of eliminating someone. You need to know the truth. This is a performance, so act as if—

"You ready, Mr. D?" Gabriel was striding toward him. Michael stood in the doorway.

He dabbed his napkin on his mouth. "Yes, just finishing up. Ready whenever you are."

Gabriel looked at George's plate, still loaded with food. "Mr. D, you barely made a dent. Nothing wrong, I hope?"

"Maybe his eyes were bigger than his stomach," Michael offered.

"No, no, it's delicious. Guess I've got a lot on my mind. Please don't tell Mr. B—that is, Carmine—I didn't enjoy it. I want to stay on his good side."

Gabriel glanced at Michael. Both men chuckled throatily. "That's always a good idea," said Gabriel.

George followed the men into a conference room where Carmine was saying goodbye to a group of meticulously attired gentlemen. George was introduced as Mr. B's physician. A few requested his business card. George was happy to oblige, pulling several from his wallet. When they left, George and Carmine sat silently facing each other across a long mahogany table that looked like something from a James Bond movie. An Apple MacBook and a gigantic white board dominated one wall; otherwise, the off-white walls were bare. Michael and Gabriel stood quietly in the background like gigantic sentinels.

Carmine loved letting the pressure build but there really was no point in frightening George. He needed his expertise.

He smiled as he closed the MacBook in front of him. "No comment about my weight or appearance? Is everything all right?"

"Yes, everything's fine." It was a relief to get started. "I have the information on the financial and health requirements for your wife's insurance and treatment if this turns out to be breast cancer. Here they are." George handed Carmine a folder with several pages containing all the information. "I wanted you to see what is required. After you look things over, I can answer any questions you have and tell you what I think your best option is. We're talking about significant choices here. Of course, I can advise you better after I examine your wife and have all the facts."

Carmine scanned the pages. George added, "I might add that if, due to risk factors, you are interested in estate taxes, I can tell you the things I've done for my fam—"

Carmine's firm grip on his hand stopped him cold.

"George, I have more advisors then I need. I want medical information, that's all. Stop all this insurance crap. Sit back and relax while I look things over." Carmine continued to pore over the documents. "I don't see any problems in the medical area. My wife is as healthy as a horse."

George told him which treatment choices he favored from his experience and made no additional comments.

"George, I know what our choice is. Before we finish up our business the boys tell me you want to discuss something personal with me. If you recall, at our previous meeting, I mentioned that I also wanted to discuss some health plan policy options with you."

Carmine had to laugh at some of the crazy requests people asked of him, legal and illegal, and was expecting something off the wall from George too.

"I'd prefer to discuss what I have to say to you alone."

"I don't see anyone else in the room, George."

"I mean Michael and Gabriel..."

"I have faith in them. The people you can't trust are the ones who have relationships based upon fear. They'll turn on you in a minute. At this moment I sense fear. Come on, George, spill it. What's on your mind?"

Carmine signaled to Gabriel, who was standing behind George. Gabriel produced from his jacket's inside pocket what looked like an ordinary fountain pen and held it in his hand.

George knew he had to sound sincere to get Carmine to commit himself. "I'm very nervous, but I'm going to have faith and tell it as I see it. I must speak from my heart or I'll never be at peace with myself. I feel like my head is about to explode.

"With all due respect, Carmine, I'm very suspicious of your motivation. If your only interest was in doing the right thing, I think you'd take my advice. I can't help but believe you are planning to eliminate your wife, with me as your weapon. I have no idea what your reasons are, but I presume our talks are because you want to insure her so you can benefit financially."

George felt a sense of power as he opened up, even if he couldn't use the word murder. He was so absorbed in what he was saying that he didn't notice Michael and Gabriel moving toward him from behind, only to be waved back by Carmine. Carmine had his reasons for letting George go on and continue his trance-like, rapid fire delivery while staring at his trembling fingers, toying restlessly with the gem clip on the medical documents.

"Why do I have this feeling, and why am I taking this risk?" he continued. "Your choices don't make sense, and I can't help but be suspicious of you and your lifestyle. I also think I can recognize in you the same desire that exists in some men: to be a free man. No more divorces and no more problems. Just a nice neat ending with many advantages.

"I've been considering ways of eliminating my wife, who's well insured. I've been working on several scenarios, the best being, to my mind an auto accident, which I could set up. But then I began to think about the possible risks if it wasn't done right. My business is caring for people, not eliminating them.

"On the other hand, your business does include a certain amount of…well, skullduggery. For instance, Bugsy Benjamin disappears and whose name comes up? Yours. *I'm* not accusing you, but… I know, I know. I'm rambling. What I'm trying to say is, I'd like to suggest we team up. I provide you with whatever you need and promise to keep all our dealings private, and you help me meet my needs in return. We each benefit and end up free of a common problem."

Carmine steepled his immaculately manicured fingers and chose his words carefully. "George, the Yellow Pages are full of surgeons. Why should I trust you? How do I know you're not wired by the police right now? Wouldn't they love a tape of me discussing eliminating our wives?"

George raised his head. "I'll strip. You can search me. I'm confused and desperate and have made my decision. Now I'm waiting for an answer. If you agree, I'm your man. I pledge to never speak a word that could cause you trouble. You can have faith in my word. It is like an insurance policy with no riders. And I'll tell you something else I've been wondering. If the Yellow Pages are full of surgeons, then why pick me? I have a sneaking suspicion that you knew damn well about my life and marriage. You've done your homework; I'm sure you have a thick dossier on ole George Dingfelder. I wouldn't risk my life by telling this to you, if I didn't think it all made sense. If I'm right, the whole scenario will look a lot less suspicious."

"George, although I admire your honesty, you sound like a very troubled man. Are you willing to proceed with the surgery, or is that contingent upon our agreeing to all the terms you have outlined?"

"Business is business. I'll get the scheduling started. I swear that no matter what develops, I won't discuss what has been said here with anyone. I presume I can expect the same of you?"

"This is only between the two of us, George. You can count on Michael and Gabriel's discretion as well. I'll pass the information on to my wife when things are set up. I think she'll go for the lumpectomy. The two of you can work it out when you see her."

"You said you wanted to ask me something about an HMO, too, before we finished."

"With this new issue before us that can wait. Michael will escort you back to the limo. You've given me something to think about. You'll hear from me shortly on your proposal. If I agree to continue to work with you, I'll want to know, as soon as possible, about appointments for my wife's preoperative medical exams. Any necessary forms to be filled out can be left with Michael or Gabriel. Good day, George."

George pushed back his chair and rose. "Good day, Carmine."

When George and Michael had exited, Carmine looked at Gabriel and said, "Got it?"

Using a USB cable, Gabriel plugged the spy pen into the MacBook. The audio opened in iTunes. Carmine's conversation with George played with crystal clarity.

———— ✳ ————

George waited impatiently for Carmine's call. He pounced on the phone every time it rang. Honey was very anxious about his behavior and kept suggesting they get away. Her call to Eunice hadn't revealed anything except that Eunice agreed with her about George's behavior.

The two wives had arranged a luncheon meeting. It was the first time they had something in common, and it helped Honey not feel guilty. She had worried that her being happily married to George was a problem for Eunice but now that they both were unhappy, she and Eunice could compare notes, diagnose George, and work together.

The ringing phone interrupted her thoughts.

George raced across the room, but Honey had already answered.

"I told you I'd get it!" he yelled.

"I live here too. It's someone named Michael. He wants to talk to you."

"Put it on hold. I'll take it in the den."

"Michael?"

"Yes, Mr. B is ready to finalize your business plans. The limo can be at your door in an hour if that's okay."

"Fine. I'll be waiting. Beep the horn. I'll come right out."

An hour later George saw the limo pull into his driveway. "Honey, I'm going out now."

When Gabriel opened the door to the passenger compartment George was surprised to see Carmine, enjoying a martini from the bar, waiting for him. George climbed in and Gabriel closed the door. Michael smiled at George from the driver's seat as Gabriel eased his beefy frame into the front passenger seat. The partition was open.

"Martini, George?" asked Carmine.

"Thanks, but it's too early for me."

"Hah! It's never too early for a martini. George, some things I do not talk about over the phone. I have a mutually beneficial plan. Tell me what you think. We all go away for a long weekend to a Vermont inn I am part owner of and—"

"That's a great idea! My wife has been concerned about my mood and just the other day suggested we take a few days off and leave the kids with her brother. Your idea fits in perfectly. No one will be suspicious."

George went on animatedly. "If the women are involved in an accident over the weekend it solves a lot of problems and looks a lot less suspicious. Separate incidents might make the police suspicious, but if the two women are off together and an accident occurs, who would suspect us? They certainly aren't going to think you'd have any reason to eliminate my wife. It would only attract attention to you—something you don't need—and I have nothing to gain but trouble by eliminating yours. So, the most likely scenario is that it's one of those unfortunate accidents that sometimes happen to nice people while they're on vacation."

"George, your kids will remain home. Where children are concerned... Well, I can't tell you how strongly I feel about protecting children and if I ever find out that you—"

"You don't have to worry about the kids. I'll see that they are taken care of. Honey has plenty of family."

"You call your wife Honey and yet you want to eliminate her."

"That's her nickname, Carmine, not a term of endearment. It confuses everybody."

"Then we'll proceed with our plans for the weekend." Carmine hoisted his martini glass. "Cheers, George. Be seein' ya."

George stepped out of the limo and Michael pulled away from the curb.

"There is one mixed up dude," Carmine remarked. "He didn't let me finish a sentence. I presume you got it all."

Gabriel held up his spy pen in the open partition.

"He must have one hell of a marriage if he thinks every man who insures his wife would like to see her dead."

Carmine wasn't smiling as he gazed into space. "Maybe it's me. I seem to bring out the worst in people. What the hell is the matter with them? My life is not a movie or TV show. I'm a businessman. I wonder where I'd be today if I'd just listened to my father. But my grandfather impressed me, and mowing lawns didn't. Everyone respected him. It was natural to want to be like him."

He pulled a crucifix on a gold chain from underneath his shirt and held it in his palm. "He gave me this crucifix to wear at my first communion. But how do you fit faith in the Lord into what my grandfather was doing? I realize now my dad wasn't anybody, but he spent his life making the world beautiful. Easy to see how he and the Lord were working together. I know how I'd feel if Junior were making the same choice today but it's too late to go back. It's done. I can't change the past. I need to decide how to use it or abandon it."

His eyes came back into focus. "To get back to business, our recording of George's plans should simplify things, open some nice business opportunities and save me a bundle. I knew he had problems and was planning on making him a cash offer. Now the offer won't cost a penny. We've got him by the balls.

"When I have the two of them up in Vermont, I'll play the tapes for him. If he refuses my offer, his wife gets to hear them. If he agrees, we go ahead with our plans. I already have the HMO lined up, and with our own medical director we're home free. Once he sees how my health plan solves his financial problems he'll cooperate and decide he can put up with his wife."

CHAPTER 12

As soon as George stepped out of the limo, he started rethinking his wedding vows and second-guessing what he was planning. Was he being crazy doing this when he could just walk away and begin a new life with Honey? Was he acting just like the people who troubled him? Should he notify the police, and what should he tell Honey to protect her? He didn't become a surgeon to kill with a knife but to heal with one. He knew ending someone's life was not something he could ever do and needed to think and work this all out.

George went directly to his office to calm himself before letting Honey know he was home. When he felt ready, he went to the kitchen, where she was preparing dinner. He could see by her expression how confused and hurt she was. She started to speak but restrained herself.

"Did you want to say something?"

"No, not now. How was your meeting?"

"As a matter of fact, you'll love this. My celebrity client is part owner of an inn in Vermont and invited us up for a long weekend. You'll get to meet him and take the break you've been wanting."

"I wish it were longer, but at least it's something. George, you seem distant. When you don't share what's on your mind, how do you think I feel? I'm your wife. I'm committed to our relationship, but I feel like you aren't letting me into your life. If there's something you've done or that has happened, please share it with me. I love you and it may help if you share it with me. Whatever it is, I'm sure two people who care about each other can work it out. Silence is not the answer. It will kill our marriage. We need to talk or go for counseling."

George listened instead of leaving the room, as he usually did whenever she tried to speak candidly to him. Honey felt encouraged.

"George, I know how you feel about marriage counseling but if we could just spend time together, away from your work and the house and kids, I think we could find something special again in our marriage.

"I know I have problems. We all do. George, I love you. You've got to believe that or there is no reason for us to go on. I don't know what your feelings are anymore. Your silence scares me, and for the first time ever I feel frightened by your behavior.

"I'm glad we're going to be doing something this weekend but it's still not what I had in mind. I wanted us to be alone. Will you at least consider what I have asked for and talk to me about it? I don't know where our marriage is headed. The man I married moved out. You're like a stranger. I know you have problems. You do a lot for all of us. I see what it takes out of you and I'm ready to help. I know I have habits that drive you crazy. I really will try to turn off the lights, the water, and the TV when I leave a room, and I'll smoke outdoors. I'm not impossible. I'll even move the cats' litter box and get clumping litter to show I love you. Shit, George, I might even stop smoking someday. I know you have a lot of anger stored up in you, but I don't see a divorce as the solution."

She idly tapped a wooden spatula against her palm while George sat at the kitchen table, wringing his hands, and mulling how best how to answer her.

"Honey I have needs too," he said at length, "and I have years of anger built up inside of me that need to come out in a healthy, non-destructive way. But how am I going to do that with all the craziness going on?"

"Maybe you're just worn out and need a rest from your practice instead of giving all the time. But if you don't tell me your needs, how can I help? I prefer anger and noise to silence. I'm frightened by what I don't know, so please, share your feelings. What you keep bottled up will kill our marriage. Two strands can bear a weight that might break one."

George had not intended to let her go on, but he had so much on his mind he was less guarded than usual. He stood up from the table to leave but lingered a moment, knowing he needed to say something.

"Thanks Honey, I know you love me, or you wouldn't care whether I used sunscreen, but you drive me nuts. I need to work on that with Hokmah. Let's see how the weekend goes and go on from there."

He had stayed, listened, and answered. The next few days passed quickly with both feeling better. George had to attend an out-of-town medical education credit meeting, which made it easier.

He knew he really had nothing to go on. He had no idea what Carmine had planned and wanted Carmine to commit himself so he could bargain with him by offering his services, even if outside the law, so they could both profit from their relationship. And if that didn't work, he still had other options. The change in Honey made him think seriously about letting her in on his plan to use her to trick Carmine into admitting he planned to kill his wife. Her being a part of it would make it much easier.

Honey worked out their schedule. Thursday George would come home early and get their things ready to put in the Suburban while she ran the kids over to her brother's place. Then they would finish packing and leave for the inn, arriving in time for dinner.

Thursday George came home as planned, changed his clothes, and went to get the bike carrier out of the garage. George had just finished attaching it to the rear bumper when Honey came out of the house.

"I'll be back shortly," she said. "Is there anything I need to pick up before we leave?"

"No, I'm all set. I just need to get that broken branch off the roof and clean the gutters before we go. The forecast is for rain, and I don't want the basement flooded again."

"Please be careful. I don't want anything to spoil the weekend. And don't forget to pack the sunscreen." She smiled and blew him a kiss.

George finished loading the bikes on the rack, put the tennis racquets inside the Suburban's cargo area, and went into the garage to get the extension ladder. He set the base of the ladder on the driveway, leaning it securely against the edge of the roof in front of the garage. He remembered Honey's warning but was in too much of a hurry to walk around the garage and position the ladder on the soft ground where the roof was lower. He climbed onto the roof, cleaned the gutters, and turned his attention to the broken limb. The branch had not completely broken off and George's twisting and tugging did no good. Like everything he did, George was a stickler for detail, he had to do it right and needed a saw.

He looked to see if Honey had returned. When he didn't see her car, he walked back across the roof, turned slowly, and carefully placed his foot on the top wooden rung which snapped as he shifted his weight onto it.

"Oh, shit!"

He was amazed how wise he became in the seconds before his body and head hit the pavement and all thinking ceased.

Returning home from dropping off the kids, Honey was excited about their chance to finally get away as she drove up their driveway. Even if it weren't just the two of them, they would have time to talk while driving. As she pulled up, she saw the ladder leaning against the house at an odd angle, George's limp body on the pavement, and the blood. She jumped from the car screaming and took his face in her hands.

"George! George! Oh my God! Someone help me!"

There was no response from George to her touch or her voice. She ran to the car to get her cell phone just as her next-door neighbor, a retired doctor, bounded through the bushes that separated their yards.

"Charlie, thank heaven you're here. I just called 911."

"Honey, don't move him. It might aggravate his injuries." Charlie knelt beside George. "His pulse is regular. His airway is clear. I'll wait with you until the ambulance arrives. Get me something to put on his head wound."

Honey scurried into the house and returned with a clean towel, which Charlie expertly applied. The blaring siren told them help was not far off.

"Over here!" Waving frantically, Honey ran toward the ambulance that appeared at the top of the driveway. Two EMTs sprang out.

"What happened?" the driver asked Honey. His partner attended to George, with Charlie bringing him up to speed.

"I don't know. My husband was going to clean the gutters before we went away for the weekend. I can only presume he fell off the roof while I was dropping the kids off."

Charlie spoke up. "I just took a quick look at the ladder and the top rung is broken. He must have fallen when it broke."

They all glanced at the ladder.

"We're taking him to the Danbury Hospital ER," said the EMT. "I need his name and age. Anything about his medical history we should know? Is he on any medications? Allergies, specific illnesses, operations?

"His name is George Dingfelder. He's thirty-seven and in very good health. Oh, he's allergic to Azithromycin."

"Got it. Thank you, ma'am."

The technicians placed a neck brace on George, started an IV, bandaged his scalp laceration, and lifted him onto the stretcher.

"Follow us to the ER," said the driver. "They'll need you there but don't speed. He's stable, so please don't get into an accident on the way. If you're too upset, get someone to do the driving."

"I can take you," Charlie volunteered.

"Thanks, Charlie, you've already done enough. I'll call my brother."

Ten minutes later her brother Doug picked Honey up. On the drive to Danbury Hospital she filled him on what had happened. When they arrived at the ER George was surrounded by aides, nurses, and doctors drawing blood and giving orders. Honey could hear them talking about his unresponsiveness.

She tried to get someone's attention, but they were all involved in his care. She waited anxiously until a doctor stepped through the curtain." Any members of the Dingfelder family here?"

"Yes, I'm his wife and this is my brother, Doug."

"I'm Dr. Gray, the neurosurgery resident. Please come with me." He led them to the family lounge littered with coffee cups and paper plates. "We can talk here without all the noise and commotion. Mrs. Dingfelder, may I call you Mrs. D?" Honey nodded yes. "Your husband has sustained significant trauma to his brain. What will need to be done and the effects it will have I can't say right now. We need to get some tests to evaluate the full extent of his injuries. Then we'll know whether surgery is indicated or just continued observation. He moves all his extremities in response to painful stimuli, so we don't believe he has a spinal cord injury. The films and scans will give us the complete picture. I know this is a difficult time for you. Do you have any questions, Mrs. D?"

"Will he wake up? Will he be alright?"

"I don't have the answer. At this point, I'd say let's hope for the best and within the hour we'll have more information. Then we'll know what to be concerned about and what our next move will be. He'll be going to the X-ray department for scans and X-rays. A nurse will go with him. I'd suggest the two of you go to the cafeteria and get some nourishment. It's going to be a long night. The attending neurosurgeon is on the way in. He'll want to see you both and go over the test results with you."

Honey was allowed to see George for a minute before he went to the X-ray department. He did not respond to her words, touch, or kiss. She was devastated. Dr. Gray tried to comfort her. She and Doug went to the cafeteria. Neither ate anything as things were too uncertain.

When they returned to the ER, George was still in X-ray. An hour later word came down that he was going directly to the neurosurgical intensive care unit. Doug and Honey were directed to the NICU family room.

After fifteen minutes, which seemed like an eternity, Dr. Gray came in with an older man.

"Mrs. D, this is Dr. Newman, our attending on-call neurosurgeon. He'll oversee your husband's care."

Dr. Gray excused himself as Newman sat down next to Honey. "Mrs. D, let me explain what his tests reveal." He held Honey's hand and looked into her eyes. She was surprised by his warmth and concern. She didn't know if this was his way of preparing her for the worst or whether he really cared.

"Your husband has no evidence of any spine or long bone fractures, and there is no sign of spinal cord injury or other soft tissue injuries. He has, however, sustained a non-displaced skull fracture and severe trauma to his brain due to the force of the fall. We do not see any sign of significant intracranial bleeding, but as with any bruised organ, swelling occurs after the injury, and that is our problem. The skull is fixed and rigid and doesn't allow room for swelling. So, his brain is under pressure. In a sense, it's as if someone was squeezing it and your husband is showing signs of increased intracranial pressure. If it reaches a critical point surgical decompression will be necessary.

Usually it will respond to the treatment he is already receiving to reduce the swelling. The most important thing we can do right now is watch him closely.

"Rather than sitting here or the cafeteria, I'd suggest you wait in the chapel. It's quiet there; prayer can't hurt, and some studies suggest it helps. If it will comfort you, I'm sure the hospital chaplain or one of the social workers would be happy to come by and do what they can to assist."

"Thank you, Dr. Newman, for taking the time to explain everything. I don't know what I need right now. I'm numb. One minute we're going away for a few days and the next…" Honey's voice faded. She could not control her emotions any longer. "Oh, God, why did this have to happen to us?"

Doug held her as she sobbed uncontrollably. The expressions of the other visitors let them know they were among people who cared. They were all stranded on the high seas hoping someone would rescue them. Your fate was no longer in your hands and you didn't feel comfortable leaving things to God. Doug said later he knew what the passengers on the *Titanic* felt like.

CHAPTER 13

Carmine, his wife Maria, and their guests waited patiently for the Dingfelders. Maria was used to his weekend meetings, though this one sounded less businesslike and she hoped they might find some time to relax and enjoy themselves. She still had hopes of coaxing Carmine into the new jogging outfit she gave him for his birthday and going out with her for a run.

When George and Honey failed to appear for dinner, they initially blamed heavy traffic. But when dinner was over and there was still no sign or call, Carmine asked Michael to look into it.

"Do you think he got cold feet, boss?"

"George is kinda squirrely but I doubt it. Still, one never knows who can be trusted until they are put to the test. The only thing we can do is call. So, get on the phone and see if anyone answers at their house. I'll wait in the lounge."

Michael dialed the Dingfelders' number from his room.

"Hello, Doug, what's happening?" answered a female voice.

"Excuse me; I'm not sure I have the right number. I'm looking for George Dingfelder."

"You have the right number. This is his sister-in-law, Rose. How can I help you?"

"I'm an associate of Mr. Dingfelder's, calling from Vermont. We were expecting George and his wife for dinner. Do you know where they are?"

"Oh, I thought you were my husband calling from the hospital. I'd forgotten about George and Honey's weekend plans in all the chaos."

"Chaos, ma'am?"

"Yes. You see, George was doing something on the roof before leaving to meet you and the ladder he was using broke. He fell and hit his head on the pavement and was taken to the hospital by ambulance. It is apparently quite serious. I'm here with the children waiting for news."

"Do you know which hospital they took him to?"

"Yes, Danbury Community."

"I hope everything will be alright. Let me leave our number with you. We want to help in any way we can."

Michael came back and motioned to Carmine, who excused himself from the group he was with. They went into the library for privacy. Gabriel joined them.

"What did you find out? Where are they?"

"Sounds interesting. Whether it's true or not I don't know."

"What do you mean?"

"His sister-in-law answered the phone. She said she's there watching the children. Apparently Dingfelder fell off a ladder and is at Danbury Hospital, in serious condition. His wife and brother-in-law are there but haven't called to give her more details. When I called, she thought it was her husband calling from the hospital. Do you think this is true?"

"Yes, I do. First, I doubt that George would cook up a scheme like this and involve his whole family. Second, did either you or Gabriel have anything to do with this so-called accident, thinking you'd be doing me a favor?" He looked Michael and Gabriel in the eye.

"No, no, we had nothing to do with it," said Michael.

"Yeah, boss," Gabriel concurred. "We work for you and don't do things without your okay. You know you can trust us."

"We wouldn't do anything crazy," they said almost in perfect unison. Surprised by this synchronicity, they looked and each other, and then back at Carmine.

The words of loyalty poured out of the lugs with such sincerity, like two kids trying to assure him they hadn't misbehaved and embarrassed the family, that Carmine was impressed.

"Boss, why would you even question us?" asked Michael. He and Gabriel looked genuinely hurt.

Carmine smiled. "I'll tell you why I had to ask you two clowns. Because I tend to think of you two when something strange happens. Ever since Luigi Forgione ended up covered with soot instead of departing this earth." He shook his head. "You two geniuses think you're doing me a favor so you tie him up in his car, start the engine, close the garage—and what happens when you come back later to untie him and make it look like a suicide? I have to apologize and buy him a new suit. If the car's a diesel you don't croak from the fumes, you just get filthy."

Michael and Gabriel gazed at the floor and shuffled their feet like naughty schoolboys.

"Now, get me the hospital's number. I want to talk with George's wife. There may be things we need to do but first I have to know his condition."

CHAPTER 14

"Mr. Dingfelder has been admitted to the NICU," the hospital dispatcher informed Michael. "I cannot discuss his condition, but I can connect you with the nurse's station."

"I'm calling about George Dingfelder. Is there anyone there I can speak to?"

"Hold on, we'll transfer you to the visitors' room."

"Hello, Mrs. Dingfelder?"

"One minute. I'll see if she's here." Michael heard her name being called.

"Yes?"

"Mrs. D, this is Michael, an associate of Mr. Birsamatto, the man who invited you to Vermont. He'd like to talk to you for a minute if that's possible."

"Please put him on. I feel awful about not calling but it's just been crazy. I haven't been able to think about anything but George."

"Mrs. D, Carmine Birsamatto speaking. I was terribly upset to hear about George. How is he? I'm no doctor but I may be able to help."

Honey explained what had happened and the risks involved. She mentioned Dr. Newman was his neurosurgeon.

"He has an excellent reputation. The reason I said I may be able to help is that I'm on the board at St. Luke's. Newman's on the staff. And I know the chief administrator, Sister Virginia Anne. With your permission and Newman's okay, I'd like to see George cared for there. They'd treat him like family. If it's all right with you, I'll talk to Newman about it."

"One minute, he's examining George. I'll see if I can get him to the phone. Can you hold on?"

"Of course."

Honey returned to the ICU. "How is he?"

"Stable—a good sign at this point," said Newman. "The next few hours are the most critical ones."

"There's a patient and friend of George's on the phone, a Mr. Birsamatto, who knows you from St. Luke's. We were to spend the weekend in Vermont with him and his wife before all this happened. He'd like to talk to you about moving George to St. Luke's. We still want you to be his doctor, but Mr. Birsamatto said he knows everyone there and would see that George got special attention. If it would make a difference in George's care, I'd like to see him moved. I'm no doctor; it's your decision. I don't want to be a pest, but I do want whatever is best for George. We have excellent medical coverage, and I don't want to have any regrets about something we should have done and didn't."

Newman's eyebrows shot up. Yes, he knew Birsamatto from St. Luke's annual fundraising banquet, not to mention his frequent appearances on the evening news. The reasons for Carmine's interest in Dingfelder's well-being weren't his concern. He followed Honey to the family room, picked up the phone, and explained the injury in layman's terms to Carmine. They talked for several minutes.

When he got off the phone he turned to Honey and said, "Any transfer at this time is out of the question, but if George's condition stabilizes, I will consider it. I don't want anyone to feel George is not getting the best treatment possible. Mrs. D—"

"I'd prefer if you'd call me Honey."

Newman smiled. "Honey, I suggest you spend some time with George now and then get some rest. People hear you even in coma, so keep talking to him and encouraging him. Even if there is no response it doesn't mean he hasn't heard you."

"I'd like to spend the night here. I wouldn't get any rest at home. I'd just worry. Can I sit with George in ICU? Sitting in the family room is torture."

"I'll talk to the nurses. They'll let you stay with him except when it interferes with his treatment. Wait here, and I'll have a nurse call you when it's okay to come in. They're catheterizing him now."

Honey spent the night at George's side, talking to him, massaging his hands and feet, sleeping for short periods with her head on the bed, or pacing the family room floor when the nurses needed to tend to him for one reason or another. Doug went home to feed the animals, walk the dogs, and help Rose babysit the kids.

Honey was awakened by Newman's hand on her shoulder.

"Good morning, Honey. After I examine George, I'll come out to the family room and we can talk." Honey rose half asleep, nodded, and left for the family room.

All eyes followed her down the hallway. Those who had experienced a loss or illness learned difficulties were a part of life and stopped running away from what they couldn't cure. It wasn't fair or unfair, just life. The rest stopped feeling and died inside.

Newman had learned the hard way when his seven-year-old son died of cancer. His feelings of guilt and helplessness devastated him and almost ruined his marriage. He and his wife had struggled to rebuild their relationship and restore some sense of normalcy for themselves and their four children after their son's death. He realized he had medical information but not a medical education which would have prepared him for the experience.

His loss changed him as a family man and physician. The nurses loved working with him because he cared for people, didn't just treat their diseases, and accepted the nurses' constructive criticism and coaching.

When Newman finished examining George, he went to the family room, sat down, and placed his hand on Honey's shoulder.

"The good news is your husband's condition remains stable. I don't see any need for surgical decompression. But I am concerned about his level of consciousness. The longer he remains in a coma the poorer the chances are of his coming out. It's still early but I have to share this concern with you."

Honey nodded. What could she say? Words held no meaning and events were beyond her control.

"Is there anything else you could do for him? Any treatments or drugs? My brother could go on the internet and—"

"If I thought there were treatments available somewhere that would help your husband, I would pursue them. Believe me, I know your pain. All we can do is the hardest thing of all: wait. I suggest you spend time in the chapel. It can help you and George. Please don't think God has anything to do with this. In my religion disease represents a loss of health, not punishment by God. We are all trying to see if we can find ways of restoring what George has lost."

Newman rose. "I'll be back later, on rounds. If I don't see you, I'll call the house."

Honey's face was buried in her hands. He touched her shoulder to get her attention.

"I speak from experience when I say stop seeing this as the end of the George you knew. It is the beginning of a situation you must learn to live with. My experience has taught me to live one day at a time and to stop picturing a negative future. We don't know what the future will be. So, live with a hopeful vision. Negative beliefs are more likely to create a negative outcome. They affect our body's ability to heal. Now, please go get some rest so you don't make yourself sick. Faith heals."

"Thank you, Dr. Newman, but, oh God, I can't leave now. My brother is coming with a change of clothing and he's bringing the children. Maybe George will respond to our kids. Oh, what about the transfer?"

"I can't say I'd recommend one hospital over the other, but I don't see it causing any added risk. He has stabilized rapidly. A good sign and if you want me to, I'll get the transfer started. We can probably move him tomorrow."

"Yes, please. I want to be sure George has the best care. Everyone here has been very concerned and kind, but Mr. Birsamatto made it sound like George would be treated like family there." Newman didn't disagree.

Carmine and Maria returned to Connecticut on Sunday and called the hospital. He told Honey he would stop by to visit the next day. He also called Newman's office to thank him. Honey had no objection to Newman keeping him informed.

Honey hoped the visits would help. She had read about a man who had come out of a coma when his grandson climbed on his ICU bed and said, "I love you, Appa." On another occasion, a boy had awakened when his puppy was placed on his bed.

George showed no response to his family, and the nurses' notes revealed he became even less responsive when his present or former wife visited. It said a lot to the nurses about the status of his present and past marriage. Something they were used to noticing.

The transfer was uneventful. Carmine's associates stopped by regularly to monitor his responsiveness and were impressed by Honey's concern.

Honey and his former wife Eunice developed an appreciation for what George had been going through now that the finances were in their hands. They thanked God for his disability insurance which the kids had nicknamed his Dizzy Billy insurance.

Carmine put his plans on hold and often brought Maria with him to make his visits look personal, knowing his actions were always under observation. He was as good as his word and had private duty nurses assigned around the clock. As George's condition showed little change, Michael or Gabriel were sent to evaluate his state of consciousness while Carmine checked in with Newman. He knew it would be easy to eliminate George and many of his associates strongly suggested it.

Carmine's associates were concerned. "We can't see any reason to take on the added risk of that idiot fabricating some incriminating story to anyone based upon his erroneous beliefs. Why do you give a shit?"

"I prefer to not carry out business activities that will upset the sisters," Carmine replied, "and I don't like kids losing their father a second time."

Carmine was moved in ways even he couldn't understand when families and children were involved.

When George's swallowing reflex returned, he was transferred to a private room. Carmine made sure the private duty nursing continued. However, George's state of consciousness showed little improvement. He was aware of people but did not respond to them.

Honey, Eunice, and their kids scheduled visits so George would almost always have someone talking or reading to him. As his ability to swallow improved they were allowed to feed him, and when they couldn't be at his bedside, they left tape recordings for the nurses to play. The nurses never played the wives' recordings while feeding him, because he became less responsive and more likely to aspirate. He responded best to the tape on which his dogs were heard barking in the background.

Newman made daily rounds and did all he could to support Honey and provide hope. He knew how important it was. Michael and Gabriel became a part of the family and often helped get George up for his feedings or into a wheelchair for a change of scenery. Carmine instructed them to be available and assist whenever needed. His motives were not entirely altruistic. He had his feelings but was wary of George waking from his semi-comatose state and sharing information that could create a problem. He didn't need any conspiracy to commit murder charges thrown at him, on top of his other legal problems. Many of Carmine's associates were not happy with his decision. It made no sense to them to not terminate the situation.

With no change in George's condition Carmine felt much less threatened and concerned. His business associates stopped discussing George. They sensed it was a personal issue and since it didn't involve them, they let the matter drop.

Even Carmine wasn't sure why the family's loss troubled him so deeply. He truly wanted to be as helpful as possible. Maria remarked to Honey and Eunice she'd seen a side of Carmine he'd never displayed before.

Even Carmine felt troubled by all the emotions which had come to the surface because of George's accident. In the past he had always tried to stop feeling and just get his thinking done, but this was different. He intuitively knew something was brewing inside of him and that he needed help too. He would make sure he and Jon discussed this at their next session so that whatever was buried in his memory would be brought to the surface and dealt with. Intellectually it didn't make sense at all, but he knew it did emotionally.

Newman scheduled a family conference to share his thoughts. "In my experience, a case like George's is very unlikely to show any dramatic improvement. With rehab, improvement may occur, but I'm not very optimistic. I think it's time to transfer him to a chronic care facility where a long-term treatment plan can be formulated. Perhaps something closer to home to make it easier for all of you."

He was about to recommend some rehab centers when Carmine, who had come to see George, spoke up. "Excuse me, Honey, but I'd like to see George remain here so we can keep his care personal. St. Luke's has an excellent rehab and long-term care center right next door, Our Lady of Perpetual Care and

Responsibility. As good as some nursing homes are …well, you've heard the horror stories, I'm sure. Our Lady's reputation is beyond reproach."

"Truthfully," said Honey, "we've gotten so used to coming here and the people that I'd prefer George stay at St. Luke's."

Newman said, "All right, I'll put his name on their waiting list and as soon as a bed—"

"I'll speak to Sister Mary Ruth in the morning and get back to you. He'll have a bed tomorrow or the next day," Carmine interjected.

Newman smiled, nodded, and thanked him. You never know when you might need a favor from a friend.

CHAPTER 15

A rehab program was started under the direction of the chief of physical medicine to train George to do all the things a child needed to learn to become independent. He responded slowly to the point where he could sit, stand, walk, and feed himself. The staff continued to notice his regression to a less independent behavior when his wives were present. Eunice and Honey had no explanation that made any sense to the staff and George wasn't talking.

Hokmah visited and gave Honey some suggestions to help stimulate and awaken George. For instance, she put photographs of the family in his room and would name and talk about each person when she visited. George showed no ability to retain the information from one visit to the next; interestingly, his memory further deteriorated when surrounded by photos of Honey.

Honey wanted George home in familiar surroundings, but it was obvious he wasn't ready, even with the help of home health aides. Everyone accepted his amnesia. There wasn't a soul who thought he was faking it.

Besides their finances, Honey now had full responsibility for the animals. Her four cats were not much of a problem. It was easy enough to leave them food and water and have the kids or neighbors empty the litter boxes, but the dogs were another story. George's three Labradors needed attention and exercise. He had built an outdoor pen for the times he was away on business trips, but this prolonged absence was taking its toll. The neighbors were used to seeing George and the three Labs running through the back roads of town; many of them volunteered to take them for walks.

But they couldn't replace George. His dogs missed him. They were listless, had no appetite, and sat in the pen staring out forlornly even when Honey or the kids opened the gate and called them. Honey knew animals were very intuitive; she was sure the dogs were aware of George's condition and not being able to see him depressed them. After reading an article in the Danbury *News-Times* about a senior citizen who died of a heart attack when he was moved into an apartment where his dog wasn't allowed, she called Hokmah.

"Honey, the best therapy for everyone would be to take the dogs to George," Hokmah advised her. "Many studies reveal the benefits of living with pets and how touching them helps raise the bonding hormones oxytocin and serotonin."

Hokmah provided several articles concerning the beneficial effects of pet therapy on diseased, handicapped, depressed, and senile patients. Honey shared the articles with Sister Mary Ruth, who talked it over with those in charge. They were concerned about dogs coming into the facility but saw no reason to restrict them from the courtyard. It was decided that after bathing the dogs and their veterinarian checking them for fleas and ticks, Honey would bring them to the courtyard. The courtyard would be closed to everyone but George and his family and the staff would take George down to visit them at the agreed upon time.

Honey was excited about the potential benefits of the meeting and arranged for an early visit. Their ten-year-old son, Carl, came along to help her, as did Eunice. The dogs were docile and cooperative, not at all the way they behaved when they were going to the vet. Honey was becoming a believer in animal communication as she watched Morphine, Valium, and Anesthesia; they had their own unique "body language." After their baths Honey had no problem getting them to enter their portable kennels. They seemed to know they were going someplace special.

When they arrived at the rehab center Honey backed the Suburban up to the courtyard entrance. She, Eunice, and Carl each walked one of the dogs towards the gate. They could see George sitting in his wheelchair wearing a helmet, staring vacantly into space.

Sister Anne Marie walked over to unlock the courtyard gate. Before she could open the gate, the dogs were upon it, yelping, whining, barking, pushing, and pulling. They had George's scent and being reunited with their master was their one and only desire. Honey's commands were disregarded and drowned out by their howling.

There are no obstacles the lover and their beloved cannot overcome. The dogs were impossible to restrain. All those present witnessed the power of love. The gate flew open before the dog's charging bodies. Honey and Eunice dropped their leashes. Poor Carl hung on and was dragged along the ground.

George turned at the sound of the barking as in they raced; howling, leashes flying, ears flapping, tongues hanging, saliva dripping straight into George's lap. The wheelchair, dogs, George, and Sister Mary Ruth became a tangled mass of love, noise, fur, and saliva. With the help of the other nuns, poor Sister Mary Ruth was able to extricate herself and the wheelchair from the tangled heap.

George lay on the ground with his three black Labs sniffing, licking, and slobbering over him. When he didn't respond they started falling over and rubbing against him. Honey had seen his head strike the ground and was concerned. It was true he was wearing a helmet, but he hadn't moved since his chair went over. And then she saw him embrace the dogs as they rolled over on him. Sobbing, he sat up, caressing, and mumbling to them as they covered him from head to toe in doggie kisses. To his dogs, George was still George because love is blind and forgives in ways amnesia never could.

Everyone stood transfixed. The nuns knelt, palms together, thanking God. Honey's tears flowed; time vanished. It was one of those rare moments when only love existed.

Dr. Newman, while on rounds, asked what all the barking was about. He was told George was in the courtyard waiting for a visit from his family and his dogs. He ran down to the courtyard.

"Is everything all right? What happened?"

Honey quickly explained what had led to their bringing the dogs in as they all continued to watch the spectacle of George and his dogs canoodling.

As Sister Mary Ruth and Newman helped George into the wheelchair, a familiar voice, no longer an unintelligible mumble, but strong and clear, could be heard above the yelping and barking.

"Come to Daddy, Morphine, Valium, Anesthesia!"

"Did you hear that?" said Honey. "He's calling them by name!"

"Come here, Morphie. Daddy loves you. You, too, Val and Annie. Come to Daddy! Where've you been? I missed you. Come here, let Daddy hold you. Give me your paw, shake hands. Roll over—I'll rub your tummy. One at a time, now, one at a time. Good boys!"

These were the first meaningful words George had uttered in two months. He rambled on and the dogs loved it. They competed for his touch and attention.

Honey, Eunice, and Carl came forward to grasp the leashes. When George was reseated, he became agitated.

"Let go of my dogs! Don't take my dogs away! Come Morphie, Val, and Annie."

"George, it's me, Honey ... your wife. Eunice and Carl are here too. Sweetheart, don't you know us?"

George lowered his voice to a ferocious whisper. "Don't touch my dogs. Don't take my dogs. They're *my* dogs. Leave my dogs alone. Somebody help me. Tell these people to go away!"

Newman stepped in. "Honey, what's happened is a great sign and opens the door for further improvement. Be thankful that a change has occurred."

"I am, but ... he seems to favor his dogs over me!"

"Honey, I'm sorry that he seems to have a closer relationship with his dogs than his family but let's be grateful for what has happened and not pass judgment. Our relationships with our pets are a lot less complex than those with our families. It's easier to be more patient and loving with animals than with spouses. It's all about living in the moment with them."

Newman's words helped Honey feel a sense of gratitude.

The dogs were finally quieted and separated. George behaved like a child whose toys had been taken away as the nuns took him to physical therapy.

Newman, Honey, and Eunice sat on the bench while Carl returned the dogs to their portable kennels one at a time, which was no easy task for a small boy. They were so energized by the meeting with George they wanted to follow him.

"Honey, this breakthrough may make it possible for George to go home," said Newman. "Let's see what happens over the next few days and how he behaves when you visit. Talk to him about how you have cared for the dogs and ask him if he would like to come home and help. We can start with day visits and gradually increase the time at home until he's ready for discharge. Does that sound okay?

"Oh, God, yes. We're not a family without him."

Because of George's improvement, two families needed to make plans.

Michael reported the changes he saw to Carmine, who learned from Newman that George's limited improvement was a hopeful sign, but no one could be sure if any further improvement would follow.

They were again dealing with uncertainty but Carmine, for the moment, stood by his decision to take no action unless George became a threat by talking about what he thought were Carmine's criminal intentions. His associates didn't agree, but it made no sense to Carmine to take risks when there was no urgency or direct threat.

Carmine reminded them he wanted to protect St. Luke's reputation, and eliminating a father was something he felt very uncomfortable doing.

The racketeer with a heart of gold only shared his sensitive feelings with Maria.

"I'm surprised by how much I appreciate the joy that George's family is experiencing," he confided to her. "I can't explain why the situation affects me so strongly. These feelings are a new experience for me. So many issues are overwhelming me in ways I never felt before. Maybe I'll start writing a journal of my feelings and share them with Jon."

For her part, Maria was thrilled beyond words with Carmine's openness about his feelings and told him so. It reminded her of the Carmine she fell in love with when they first met.

"Carmine, my love," she said, "I'm so glad you've gotten in touch with your feminine side."

There was a time when Carmine would have considered such a declaration an insult. In fact, he might have gone so far as to belt in the mouth any of his associates with the audacity to venture such an opinion. But that was the old Carmine. Carmine 2.0 was secure in his masculinity and, becoming in touch with his feminine side too; thus, he took Maria's words as a high compliment.

Accompanied by Maria, Carmine continued to visit George occasionally. He knew he was under observation by the authorities, who were still working on Benjamin's disappearance. Carmine found the observation more annoying than usual since he had no dealings with Benjamin but always seemed to be considered a suspect.

He felt certain that George's recall was limited to his dogs. He showed no awareness of their past discussions and plans. Honey and Eunice, son Carl, and daughters April and Betty all received the same response: an emotionless greeting. George was beginning to repeat words and names, as an infant does, and once in a while Honey saw a look in his eyes that suggested he was desperately trying to communicate, as if he knew what he wanted to say but couldn't pull up the correct file because the computer was down.

With time, George was able to care for himself and express his needs. Newman felt he was ready to be discharged from Our Lady of Perpetual Care and Responsibility. Honey made the necessary plans and Carmine arranged for home health aides with the Foster Agency. Patty Foster owed him a favor and her staff would provide daily reports regarding George's behavior.

When visiting George at home, Michael, Gabriel, and Carmine privately asked him a specific set of questions pertaining to their secret dealings which, far from eliciting any concrete answers, just agitated, and frustrated him. The way George was getting along with his present and former wives, Carmine felt, was an even surer sign he had no memory.

As far as Honey was concerned, amnesia was very therapeutic for their relationship. They were becoming a family again. Since George was not capable of working, he spent most of his time with the kids or helping to run the household. When the home health aides were no longer required, it was back to occasional visits by Carmine's angelic associates. Hokmah also continued to advise Honey with visits and phone calls.

Carmine envied him in some respects. It was a gift to have no past events to forgive or forget and no future to worry about. George behaved more like his dogs than a person. Here was a man who had no problem living in the moment; like kids, the aged, or those close to death he couldn't do anything wrong and didn't need to know.

Samuel Seltzer and Marvin Graham displayed a keen interest in George and wanted to learn from him, too, but not about the benefits of amnesia. The former was with the state police, the latter, the FBI. They had a common quest:

to uncover evidence incriminating Carmine and find out why he displayed such concern about George's state of health.

The state police cars had recently been repainted with the words PRIDE and PROGRESS on the hood. It was an inside joke that this was done because one officer was named Pride and the other Progress. When Seltzer and Graham teamed up, the department felt it was more fitting to call them Bubbles and Cookie. Bubbles was a tall, slim, drawling slowpoke, and Cookie, the pair's mouthpiece, was a fidgety, fast-talking New Yorker, a diminutive ball of energy. If Bubbles was Gary Cooper, Cookie was James Cagney.

Bubbles and Cookie contacted Honey and arranged to meet.

"The accident and interest by the Mafia may not be coincidental," Cookie explained to her. "George might be able to provide us with information; in return, we would grant him freedom from prosecution. We will protect your family, too, if anything does come from our investigation."

They interrogated George at Newman's office. Watching George reminded Honey of Marlon Brando stonewalling the two detectives in *On the Waterfront*. "I don' know nothin', I ain't seen nothin', I'm not sayin' nothin'. So why don' you and your girlfriend take off?"

Despite the consistency of George's responses and behavior at each of their visits, concern about the reality of George's loss of memory persisted. Could it all be an act? They'd seen the Mafia use the amnesia routine in court to deny guilt. Suspicion was the name of Bubbles' and Cookie's game. However, Judge Dunklee refused to authorize a wiretap on George and Carmine's phones for lack of incriminating evidence. He felt Carmine's interest in George was not clearly related to any criminal activity and, therefore, insufficient evidence for a wiretap. Their persistence—and Carmine's prolonged interest in George's welfare—finally raised the judge's suspicion.

"Supposing George's accident was not an accident because they wanted George eliminated?" Cookie conjectured.

"Why would they want to do that? Where's the evidence?" Dunklee argued back. "And if he were a threat to them, why would they have waited this long?"

"Maybe we can get some answers from a wiretap. Who knows what interests Carmine so much? Maybe they need to know something that George's injury made him forget and that's why they're hanging around. We can't believe they're just friends. There's got to be something more to it. Maybe it has to do with finances, drugs, or a health insurance scam."

"I'll authorize the wiretap for a six-week period but that's it."

George was blissfully unaware of the great interest in him by so many organizations and families. He spent each day enjoying his family and his dogs, playing with April during the day and helping Betty with her homework after school.

Besides running, George had a great love for baseball. Even though he had no memory of his past he still manifested a love of the game. When he wasn't helping Honey or the girls, he watched the Yankees' games on TV. They were in the thick of a pennant race. When Carl visited, they watched together.

"Carl, your dad doesn't remember but he was quite a baseball player in school," Honey remarked. "You ought to encourage him to play with you. The exercise would do him some good."

Like most ten-year-olds, Carl jumped at Honey's suggestion. They found George's old glove and Honey dropped them off at the nearby high school to take turns hitting and fielding.

Carmine's limo pulled up while they were playing.

"Honey told me I'd find you guys here. How are things going?"

"Want to play, Mr. Birsamatto?"

"No, thanks, Carl. Baseball's not my game, though I do enjoy watching it because it's not over until the last out. I don't like games where you run out of time. How're you doing, George?"

"I'm frustrated as hell but I'm trying to take things one day at a time."

They talked for a few minutes while Michael and Gabriel played catch with Carl.

"George, seeing how much the two of you enjoy baseball, I have box seats for the playoffs and World Series if the Yanks win the pennant. Would you and Carl like to come to one of the games? My grandson is coming. He and Carl would make good company for each other and the wives are invited too."

"Are you kidding? Name the day and we'll be there. Carl, did you hear what Mr. B said?"

"Yeah! Wow, thank you, sir. Wait till I tell my friends! The Yanks are going to win the pennant, Mr. Birsamatto. I just know it!"

Carl was right. The Yanks won the pennant, as he predicted, with George and Carl sitting in front of the TV set cheering. True to his word, Carmine invited them to the opening game of the World Series. Carmine decided to make a day of it, feeling visible social contact might put off any suspicion by the authorities. His business associates still felt any public display of closeness to George was a mistake. The entourage included George, Carmine, Honey, Maria, Carl, Carmine Jr., Michael, and Gabriel. The group occupied Carmine's box seats, just past the dugout on the first base side. After the game, dinner at Morelli's, Carmine's favorite Italian restaurant, was planned.

George had just one proviso. "Honey, I will absolutely not wear my helmet to the game. I find it too embarrassing."

Honey knew there was no point in arguing. Newman agreed that he should just use good sense and wear it when appropriate. George and Carl proudly wore their Yankee caps.

Carl was ecstatic when they got to the ballpark. Their seats were right on the railing next to the dugout. Carmine had suggested they come early to watch the warm-up and get some autographs. George, Carl, Carmine Jr., and Carmine sat in the front row and Michael sat on the aisle behind George with Honey, with Maria and Gabriel filling the second row. Michael and Gabriel were always anxious when Carmine was out in public and kept an eagle eye on the crowd for any sign of suspicious characters.

George started to discuss the history of Yankee Stadium with Carl, but Carl was more interested in food.

"Could I have a hot dog, Dad?"

"I don't know why not. Anyone else want one?"

"I'll take one, Mr. D," said Gabriel.

George stood up and, with his back to the field, shouted and waved to attract the vendor's attention. "Hey, hot dogs, three over here, with everything!"

The vendor came down and Gabriel took the three mustard and sauerkraut laden hot dogs. While George was reaching into his pocket to pay for them, the batter fouled off the next pitch.

All eyes followed the trajectory of the ball, hopeful of obtaining a souvenir. They were to be denied. The ball descended and, while everyone was absorbed with hot dogs, struck George squarely in the head and bounced back onto the field.

The sound of the ball striking George's skull reverberated throughout the stadium. Unlike a base hit, the sound was greeted by a wave of silence and the game became insignificant. The wise, more aware of their vulnerability, savored the moment. The unenlightened became immobilized by their whys.

Why are there accidents? What is fate? What is luck? Why did he stand up? Why do batters foul off pitches? Why did he order three hot dogs? Are there blessings, curses, and coincidences? What schedule is the universe on? Who's in charge? How could anyone understand why? Why did God make a world like this?

George tumbled into Michael, creating a sandwich of hot dogs, mustard, and sauerkraut. Michael tried to hold him but George, lubricated by condiments, slipped through his hands. The crowd grew still. Players ran over. Michael wiped his hands. Carmine stared in disbelief. Honey screamed.

George's hand slipped from hers as he collapsed into the space left by the raised seat. It was déjà vu all over again. Once again time ceased to exist, and George was the center of attention.

CHAPTER 16

Carmine stared in disbelief as Michael and Gabriel lifted George back into his seat. At the same time Honey was climbing over the seat, bellowing his name. While the players gathered at the railing, a physician seated nearby came over to offer his assistance.

George reached for his cap. "Honey, stop screaming in my ear. Calm down. I was stunned, that's all. I wasn't expecting to be hit on the head by a baseball. My head hurts, and I'm a mess. Michael, you look like you need a dry cleaner. Honey, you keep everything anyone could ever need in your purse. Give us something to wipe ourselves with."

Honey pulled out an unopened packet of moist tissues. The players tossed them towels to wipe off the remains of the hot dogs. Carl picked one off George's shirt but had lost his appetite. The vendor offered free hot dogs, but no one was hungry.

The team physician brought an ice pack from the dugout and teased George about never turning his back on anyone.

The image of George, being ministered to by the team doc and surrounded by family and friends, appeared on the Jumbotron with the caption HE'S OKAY FOLKS! The stadium erupted in deafening cheers and applause. Carmine saw himself on the Jumbotron and, leery of the unwelcome publicity, turned his back. The umpire shouted, "Play ball!" and the game resumed.

Everyone but Honey, who sensed a change in George, directed their attention back to the field; there was again time for life's meaningless distractions.

"George, how did I get my nickname?"

"Why are you asking me that now? This is no time for stories about your childhood."

Carl felt something too. "Dad, what'd you get me for my last birthday?"

"A chemistry set. Why are the two of you asking me crazy questions? We're here to watch a ball game."

George began to feel very uncomfortable, as if he were sitting at his computer watching a lost program being retrieved.

"Please stop. I just want to enjoy the game."

But the game was no longer the most interesting event of the day for those aware of the return of at least some of George's memory. Honey, Carl, Carmine, and his associates were all wondering what this would mean to them. Only George, Maria, and Junior were able to focus on the game.

The Yanks won, defeating Boston 5-3 on a last inning home run. The following day a color photograph immortalizing George, and those present in Carmine's box, appeared in every newspaper's sports section. Carl has a copy, autographed by the entire Yankee team, on his bedroom wall. Bubbles and Cookie dropped a copy off at Judge Dunklee's office.

Carmine knew the return of George's memory had to be explored carefully. Eventually he was evaluated by everyone from his neurosurgeon to his mailman. What they learned was that George displayed a combination of lost computer programs and premature senility.

Newman said he displayed a positive Goldberg test, a common evaluation to assess various mental disorders. Neither Honey nor Carmine had heard of it. Newman explained: "George is showing the typical recovery pattern. Memory which returns with the greatest clarity is of one's more distant past. As you approach the date of the trauma, the vaguer recall becomes. For a period of several weeks before the fall to the day of the game there is still a complete blank."

Honey, Eunice, and the kids spent time educating George about what he had forgotten. Doug, as his medical partner, worked with him at their office so that he could ease back into his medical practice without feeling pressured.

Carmine needed to be certain George wasn't deceiving him. Hokmah helped him to understand what was going on in George's brain and he eventually concurred with Newman's diagnosis. Carmine's business associates were tired of the distraction and unhappy about its effect on Carmine. They began to discuss ways of dealing with George, without asking Carmine, should it become necessary. They wanted Carmine's full attention focused on current business, not George.

The police and FBI were even more intrigued by his behavior and Carmine's renewed interest. They again questioned George. Bubbles and Cookie (neé Seltzer and Graham) played recordings of their past meetings to assist his memory, explaining that their interest in him pertained to his relationship with Carmine and what he knew about the racketeer's business activities.

They made it clear that if George provided them with information incriminating Carmine, they would guarantee him freedom from prosecution.

"My dealings with Carmine were all legitimate health related transactions," George assured them. "I have the records in my office. Furthermore, I'm offended by your insinuations."

His sincerity, born of amnesia, impressed them. All their questions about anything more recent George answered with his Marlon Brando imitation. In essence: "I don't know anything. I haven't seen anything. I can't remember anything." They finally gave up the questioning as futile. They realized George's memory loss was not an act. He had no recall of any criminal activity involving Carmine, and they didn't find his Marlon Brando imitation very funny.

As he resumed his family responsibilities, problems began to resurface. As the sun rises the darkness fades. Only no one knew if or when the sun would rise for George and what it would cast light on. Eunice and Honey tried to reassure him and suggested ways they could be of help.

"George, why are you up at this hour?" Honey asked him on one occasion, finding him staring out the picture window.

"I'm having crazy dreams. I was in a house and able to open all the doors except the one to the attic. And I knew there was something important stored there I needed to be aware of. Is there something you're keeping from me? Do I have a brain tumor? I have feelings I can't explain and it's getting to me."

Honey had assured him none of those dire scenarios applied and helped him back to bed.

With less sleep, George became more anxious and difficult to live and work with. He was everyone's problem. Even Carmine was becoming frustrated. The accident had aborted his plans to pressure George into participating in health care fraud. Now George represented a risk to him because of his beliefs about what was to have occurred that weekend in Vermont.

At the same time Carmine's relationships and family had become more important to him. His children and grandchildren noticed the change. Maria, who had already noted Carmine's increased sensitivity, was delighted her husband was more willing to listen these days. He resumed regular sessions with Hokmah and started bringing up issues he had kept buried since his childhood.

Despite his dangerous vocation, Carmine had never seriously considered his own mortality. People weren't assassinated, murdered, or killed. They were eliminated, taken out, or disappeared. Those acts seemed under his control. He was like a doctor who didn't get sick or die; his patients did. The word death was never used, and you kept your power by eliminating threats. He began to appreciate what he had … but who knew for how long. George reminded him that order and control are two different things.

Carmine became more aware of his struggles. He had doors that needed to be opened too. After his therapy sessions he occasionally reflected upon what was important in his life to Michael and Gabriel, much to their surprise.

"Boys, I don't have all the answers. Keep that to yourselves. I feel a need to serve now more than I need others to love or serve me. I'm beginning to understand what my father was trying to tell me."

George, due to his past experience as a doctor, found it hard to accept help. He was the chief surgeon at all times in his mind.

He tried to lose himself in his practice and keep distracted. Newman prescribed some mild tranquilizers, but Honey knew him best. She put out his sneakers and jogging outfit. George hadn't done any jogging since his injury and had forgotten how good it felt. George and his dogs started taking long walks twice a day. As he got back into shape, he resumed jogging.

Doug also prescribed some beneficial therapy. "George, I just received a brochure about a medical education meeting in Orlando. It looks interesting and would give you a chance to get away, relax, and sharpen your surgical skills all at the same time."

Once again George had the misfortune to experience one of mankind's greatest dilemmas. What occupies our thoughts: the sunshine or the darkness? What do we record in our journals: pleasant events or disturbing ones? Have you ever been to a place where there are no telephones, e-mail, fax, radio, computer, TV, mail, and newspapers? Ah, the bliss—you're in charge of your time and can reconnect at your convenience. But remember what a shock it was to come home? George was learning what it's like to recover from amnesia. Losing your memory is like taking a long vacation free of your past and where no one can reach you. Having it return is like coming home to the demands of the world.

One morning while cleaning up after breakfast George said, "Honey, remember how getting away always helped me? This conference sounds great. There are presentations about personal as well as medical relationships. They may help me reintegrate my life."

"What do you remember about our plans for the weekend in Vermont?"

"Just what you've told me. Carmine invited us up to spend the weekend. We were getting ready to leave when my accident changed everything."

George found it disturbing to discuss.

Honey looked directly at him. He didn't return her gaze. She took his hands and said, "George, George, listen to me. I want to come with you. We need to get away together, to enjoy some time away from everything and everybody—just the two of us. I can attend some sessions too. I've seen the brochures. There are events scheduled for spouses. We both can learn something. I won't be hanging onto you every minute. We never had that weekend, and I think we owe this to ourselves. We need the time, George. Our world has changed. No one's to blame, but it's up to us to try and restore it."

Honey went on in an impassioned way. Looking into her face always calmed him. He saw her the way he had when they first met. It was one of the things that had attracted him to her but that he could never completely understand or explain. He often told her it was hard for him to remain angry at her when he looked into her face.

"Honey, there's so much going on inside of me I can't understand. I need time to think and work it out. My head is a mess. Yes, I remember more and can function but something else is happening. Carmine, Seltzer, and Graham aren't helping and may be the problem. Maybe it's time for us to get away.

"It's been a long time since I've had the feeling I used to get when I look at you. It came over me just now while you were talking. It felt so good! I don't know whether it's the right thing or not for us to go away together but things can't get much worse. I'll call the travel agent. You work out getting someone to watch the creatures and the kids. I love you."

He took Honey in his arms and held her, the two of them rocking slowly back and forth. The mood was broken when April and Betty burst in crying, complaining Carl had thrown mud at them.

Honey was excited. She envisioned talking about something other than the kids' needs, George's problems, and her bad habits.

George had no expectations. He simply accepted it might help him get his life in order, and he looked forward to sharing time with Honey, free of their daily demands.

On the ride to the airport Honey rested her hand on George's neck and he reached over and touched her hair. In the airport they walked holding hands, something they hadn't done in years, unless it was to help George after his fall. When they settled into their seats Honey rested her head on George's shoulder and took a nap. They both experienced feelings they hadn't felt in a long time.

George was moved while still feeling a confusing emptiness. He didn't want to upset Honey by discussing what he didn't understand. He hoped when the door to his past opened things would change for the better. He wasn't sure it would help to have Honey along, but he knew it was important for her to come. When they returned home, he planned to see Hokmah again.

Their meeting was at Disney's Grand Floridian Resort and Spa in Orlando, a pleasant change from the often staid accommodations of typical medical conferences. The view, nice weather, and surroundings helped them unwind. Honey, outfitted in a loud flowered shirt, giant straw hat, and oversized sunglasses, acted like a typical tourist, snapping pics of everything in sight. They went over the program and decided which sessions they would attend. The first sessions oriented toward health care, only George attended. When the sessions on how relationships, work, and love affected your health began, they attended them together.

They drew pictures of their family and themselves at work and laughed at what they revealed. It felt good to laugh, and to learn from the workshop leader's interpretation of their drawings how personality characteristics—that led to success in business—also ruined marriages. In small groups they shared problems, like the onus of scooping kitty litter.

Evenings they dined and danced. Mornings they showered together, rediscovered their bodies, and made love. As they were standing naked in the bathroom one morning, George was moved when Honey reached over and removed a piece of tissue paper stuck to his cheek, leftover from cutting himself shaving. This simple gesture left him feeling accepted. More like a second honeymoon than a medical conference, the Florida trip was decidedly unlike the last few years of their marriage. They talked, touched, lived for the moment, and found what had been lost.

George appreciated that the relationship sessions were run by a married couple, considering his past, unsatisfying experience with a divorced marriage counselor. During one session the woman led them in a guided imagery. They were holding hands, something George was comfortable doing now. He squeezed Honey's hand three times, signifying "I love you." The counselor had told George and Honey what the gesture meant when she first demonstrated it, so they would understand the silent communication. Honey squeezed back three times and their hands parted.

The images were unclear, but he began to sense a feeling of grief. It was as if he were in the audience of a play, waiting for the curtain to rise but fearful of what the play was about. He sat transfixed as the events preceding the weekend came flooding back. He was no longer blind and numb. His grief and guilt could only be understood by those who have hurt someone they love.

His sobs disrupted the session. Honey whispered to him and led him out of the room, followed by the workshop leader's husband.

"This has been an enormous help," said George. "Please let everyone know that. I don't want them to worry about me. I can't discuss what happened but please thank your wife for helping me to find something I've been searching for."

The counselor reassured George that he would share his words with everyone and that he and his wife were available for consultation if needed. George and Honey returned to their room, where he lay on the bed staring at the ceiling.

"George, what happened? Can I help?"

"I need time to think. I'd appreciate it if you didn't say anything. I don't know what to say and if I say the wrong thing, I don't know what effect it will have on our marriage. It's not something you can change and it's not about anything you have done. It's about the past— something I feel is inappropriate to talk about until I have a better sense of it myself. I'd feel better if you'd leave me alone. I told you about my confusion over what I was feeling. Well, now I understand it but I need time to put things together so I can share them with you without causing more pain and problems. Please give me some time and space."

"I'll go and watch TV. Call me if you need me. I'm confused and feeling a little frightened again. I don't know who you are from one day to the next. You're like someone with a multiple personality."

Honey left while George thought about his options. Do I tell Honey anything? Should I call Carmine? What if the police find out about our deal? He had to take his chances. There was no way to evade Carmine unless he assumed a new identity. He didn't like that choice and it was no guarantee of safety. Carmine had gone along with him thus far. Maybe there was something he didn't know that had protected him besides Carmine's good will. He planned his dialogue, knowing Carmine's phone might be tapped.

"Hello, Michael, is Carmine there? I have some good news." Carmine came on the line. "Yes, George, what is it? I heard you were away."

"I am. I'm at a medical meeting in Orlando at the Grand Floridian. During one of the sessions my memory returned, and I thought you'd like to know and celebrate my recovery with me. I remembered the plans we were to finalize on the Vermont weekend. I want to thank you for not taking your business elsewhere while I couldn't function. I'd like to discuss some changes I think are indicated now that I can evaluate things again. I would like to discuss other options with you when I return."

"I'm thrilled about your recovery and look forward to our meeting. I'm glad you're able to function again. Call me when you get home."

Carmine hung up. George sat staring at the phone in his hand, wondering if he had just arranged his own murder. He had no choice. There was no place to hide. He knew by telling Carmine where he was, he could return the call from a safe phone. George felt that would be a hopeful sign because you didn't call someone you were planning to eliminate.

He heard sounds coming from the phone—telltale sounds someone was listening on the extension in the sitting room.

"Honey, how could you intrude like that? If I can't trust you how can I share anything with you?" he screamed at the closed door. When she didn't appear, he went into the sitting room and stared at her. She was in the act of placing the receiver in the cradle. "What made you do that?"

"George, I need to know something. I'm scared and I can't live this way. My life is like a roller coaster ride. I can't take it anymore. I can't live with uncertainty. I need to know what's going on or I'm getting off this ride. I'm not an idiot. I know who Carmine is and what his business is. I'm frightened by your relationship with him and the change in you. I've kept a lot of questions and concerns inside of me up till now, but I need to be in on all this so I can live and sleep without fear."

The ringing phone interrupted them.

"I think you're going to get what you asked for. I only ask that you say nothing until I'm done speaking to Carmine. Can you do that for me? Then I will speak to you and listen to what you have to say." She nodded and George went into the bedroom. He motioned to Honey to listen on the sitting room phone.

"Carmine?"

"No, Mr. D, it's Michael. We appreciate your not talking business on our phone. Mr. B wants to see you when you get home."

"Michael, I'll call as soon as we get back to set up a meeting. If that isn't okay, you can ask him if he wants you to meet us at the airport and take us to his place. It's on the way back from LaGuardia. Please tell him he has nothing to worry about. Fear is not what motivates me."

"Okay. I'll pass your words on and let you know his decision."

George hung up and went into the sitting room. "I'm sorry, Honey, I expected Carmine to be on the phone."

The intensity of her stare paralyzed him.

"I want to know what the hell is going on that is so sinister you can't talk about it over the phone. Either tell me now or when we get home, I'm out the door and I'm taking the kids with me! This is not some stupid TV reality show, George—it's real life! I don't need more problems. My life is already difficult enough."

"This may be a mistake, but we've gone too far for me to hide anything anymore. I only ask one thing of you: please listen to my entire story. So much has happened. I'm not the same man you married and lived with all these years. I see things differently and feel differently now. That's what I'm going to discuss with Carmine because the plans made this summer and the chances, I was prepared to take make no sense to me now."

"George, stop rambling and tell me something. I'll listen until you're done."

Her intensity broke the barrier. Words poured out of him as fluidly as they did when he saw Hokmah. Every few sentences he stopped to regain control of himself.

"I felt like I was dying. I felt trapped with no options, incapable of feeling anything. I had to change my life and I thought I had to eliminate something to survive. I couldn't survive another divorce so I couldn't kill the marriage, and I didn't have the guts to kill myself. I know you'll probably never understand this but I needed to have hope, and the only place I found it was in fantasizing about eliminating you and being free of all my problems, with that one step. I wasn't really thinking about doing it or planning it. I know you love me, or you wouldn't worry about my using sunscreen. My life was just so crazy it was driving me to distraction. The planning was like a game or a hobby to me. It was all a fantasy, but I felt better doing it and being creative. Like writing a book."

He described how he had met Carmine and the evolution of his thoughts and concerns about Carmine's reasons being like his, but not a fantasy. Despite George's revelations, Honey's face remained impassive. George thought his eloquence was winning her over. After pausing a moment to control his emotions, he continued.

"I beg you to forgive me so we can start over. I know you love me, and I know that what I'm asking of you will take incredible strength on your part. You must understand I'm not the old George. I finally understand that my life isn't threatened, and that love is an option which can eliminate my problems too. Please, please, Honey I beg you to act out of trust and faith in me now. Please give me a chance to truly straighten this all out. I know I can do it without hurting you or our children. I will get help. I'm putting my life on the line by sharing this with you and Carmine because I love you. I want us to be a team and have a relationship we both appreciate and desire. It will be a struggle, but I know it will be worth the effort."

"Stop, stop! I've heard enough and I don't care what I promised! I know you're not the old George anymore because now you're a total asshole!" This was a Honey he had never seen. "If you'd had an affair with another woman and asked me to forgive you and start again, because you were a changed man, I could do that. But you start out by fantasizing about killing me, George! Killing me! That means you were thinking about it and it was a real possibility. How the hell can I ever lie down next to you or let you touch me and not remember that? How do I sleep, make a meal, clean the house, and care for our children without thinking you wanted to kill me? Then you offer me as bait to a shark. This is not a movie we're discussing. This is my life! I can't switch roles to suit you. My God, you say I don't know how you felt. Well, how about how I feel now? I'm married to a man who fantasizes about ending my life! We're not talking spousal abuse George, we're talking murder. Murder, George! You put my head on the chopping block, not yours, fantasy or not. I need to get out of here before you're dead or castrated. You son of a bitch! And you have the balls to complain about my smoking!"

"Honey, let me explain. It was like I was writing a book—"

"You bastard! Shut up and listen before I do something, we'll both regret! There's nothing you can say that will change what I'm about to do. I'm getting the hell out of here so we'll both be safe. When the meeting is over, call me. I'll tell you then what I've decided. Ask Carmine if you can stay at his place when you get back. It will be safer if you have a place to go to. Now hand me the phone so I can see about being on the next plane out. I can't feel comfortable having you do anything for me or with me anymore."

That night Honey was on a plane back to New York. Needless to say, she consumed quite a few glasses of wine. She had options, too, and Carmine was one of them. She and Carmine would probably both agree to George's elimination, fantasy or not. That thought, combined with the wine, brought a smile to her lips, and she was able to rest picturing Carmine responding to her call. Maybe Carmine had a family plan with lower elimination rates. Her sick humor helped her feel less like a victim and more understanding of what George was trying to tell her about his feelings of desperation. It felt as if they had reversed roles. Now he was the troubled spouse and she the empowered one. Fantasizing was therapeutic. Maybe George had a point about fantasizing too.

CHAPTER 17

After putting Honey's bags on the airport shuttle, George walked back into the hotel lobby to reflect on the mess he had created.

He spoke to Gabriel on the phone. "Please tell Carmine that I'm in a difficult situation emotionally. My wife has gone home early, and I'd appreciate being picked up at the airport so we can connect. I'll wait to hear from you." He gave Gabriel the flight information and went for a ride on the monorail as a distraction. The contrast between his feelings and the joyful vacationers only made things worse.

At the remaining sessions, his internal dialogue drowned out the speakers. He was tired of trying to escape, but he didn't know what risks he had to take to straighten things out. He knew he was the problem and the solution.

"I need to act as if I still have amnesia. Relate to everyone as if we had no past and eliminate the old problems by behaving like a new George."

"You're no saint. How are you going to understand, forgive, and love when you don't really have amnesia? You failed before and you probably will again."

Listening to this inner conflict, he felt like he had an angel on one shoulder and a devil on the other, like in those old cartoons. Knowing he was going through a dissociative reaction, as Hokmah termed it, didn't help. All George could do was sit back and listen to the conversation of all his multiple internal personalities.

At that moment performers dressed as Mickey Mouse, Donald Duck, and Pluto passed by. George watched fascinated as children flocked to them, dancing and capering with their heroes, and even the adults fell under their spell, instantly becoming childlike.

"You need to act like a child and do your homework. If Honey coaches and trains you, and you practice being the husband she deserves to have, things can change."

He hurried back to his hotel room to call and tell Honey their future could be a joyful and loving one if they used the pain of the past to motivate them. He had to make her see the key to a new life was in their hands, and how their hunger could lead them to find a way to nourish their lives.

He called and left a message on the answering machine. "Honey, if the past was a dam blocking the flow of our life, let's burst it and use its power as a source of energy to rebuild our marriage. Please call me back. Okay? I love you."

Proud of his eloquence and brevity, he stretched out on the bed to wait for her return call, feeling more hopeful. His inner voice reminded him he had choices.

"You don't have to throw away the TV set if you don't like the program. You change channels. You have a mind; like a remote control it can select the channel that is a healthy one, and your body can then live and demonstrate the program presented."

He laughed; life is a great teacher when you stop being a victim. He scanned the movie titles and found *The Dream Team*. "That's what I need in my life. We could become the dream team."

When the movie was over, he wondered why he hadn't heard from Honey. He called Doug.

"Doug, is Honey at your place? I've been trying to reach her at the house but there's no answer."

"I have no idea where she is. She's probably resting or out shopping. Relax. The kids are here and we're expecting Honey to pick them up shortly. I'll have her call you."

His inner dialogue began again. What if she was feeling overwhelmed by their marriage and her life? She had lost her first husband and her second one put her life at risk.

He called their neighbor, Charlie Pomeroy. Charlie was a good egg; Honey had told him how the retired physician had rushed to his aid when he fell off the ladder. He was always willing to lend a helping hand.

"Charlie, sorry to bother you, but I need a favor from you."

"Shoot, George."

"Honey and I were down in Florida for a medical thing. We had a little spat and she flew back home. I'm still down here and I can't get her to answer the phone. Would you see if she's home? Tell her I'm sorry about everything. Tell her I'm desperate to talk to her. Tell her to listen to my phone message. I'm willing to do anything to make our marriage work again."

"I was a pediatrician, not a marriage counselor, George. I'm not sure I want to get involved in this."

"Come on, Charlie. I'll owe you one."

"You owe me several already. But alright I'll do it."

"Thanks, buddy."

Charlie observed that the Dingfelders' Suburban and Audi were both in the driveway; Honey was probably home. After a great deal of bell ringing and door pounding, he finally got her to the door. She had been taking a nap while wearing earplugs and was none too pleased to be awakened. Even after Charlie relayed George's message, practically verbatim, she stood with her arms folded, eyes blazing.

"Don't shoot me, Honey, I'm only the messenger. George sounded genuinely contrite." With that, Charlie took his leave.

Honey played George's phone message. His words stirred some tiny ember of love somewhere deep inside her. Against her better judgment, she called him.

"Charlie said you phoned him; he told me what you said. What is it you want from me, George? Make it quick—I've got to pick up the kids and take them to a birthday party."

George cringed at her sharp tone. "Did you listen to my phone message?"

"Yes, very poetic ... for bullshit."

"Honey, I—"

"You know, George, if you keep this up, you'll be the one in danger. It's probably easier to eliminate men then understand them. Hell, at this point I can understand why a woman would want to be a nun, and why a friend of mine got a divorce after her mastectomy. She gave up a tit and an ass. Next time you want to have dinner out I'll put a sandwich on the front porch for you, and if you ever call the missing persons bureau I hope they tell you to get lost."

"Honey, I know we can be happy together. You and your sense of humor are a treasure. I know that now. That's why I was so worried when you didn't call back. I have spent a great deal of time thinking about our future. Please meet me when I get home. Maybe at Carmine's so we can talk. The past is over. Don't hate me. Give me a chance."

"I don't hate you; I just question your sanity. It's easy for you to talk about happiness, but when the past includes your husband fantasizing putting your life at risk that could represent a minor obstacle, don't you think? How do I know that you aren't planning something right now?"

"I felt helpless, as if someone else was giving me orders. I know there are other options now. I know love can solve and eliminate our problems. I know it in my heart. You've got to believe me. What else can I say? Our future is in your hands. Love is my power and my weapon of choice now."

"When are you coming home?"

"I'm waiting to hear from Carmine about being met at the airport. I have some things I must settle with him and then I'll be home. I'll leave a message on the answering machine if I miss you."

When George hung up the phone, Bubbles and Cookie, who had been monitoring the call, exchanged a high-five. Now that they had on tape George's intention to commit murder, they had some leverage. They knew they were stretching things legally, and didn't have much of a case, but if they could get to George before he had a chance to talk to an attorney and threaten him with possible imprisonment, he might help them set up something so they could get to Carmine. They would meet George's flight, arrest him, and pressure him in the car.

George's room phone rang again. It was Gabriel. "Dominic and Constantine will be picking you up. They'll meet you in the baggage claim area."

Gabriel hung up and turned to Carmine. "Boss, why the personnel change?"

"Yeah, me and Gabe have developed a kinda copacetic relationship with Mr. D," Michael chimed in.

"I can't argue that George isn't a risk anymore. No matter what my intentions were for the weekend getaway his beliefs, phone calls, and conversations are exposing us. We have to protect ourselves. I have mixed feelings about it because of all we've been through, but business is business. I can't let our security be endangered. Taking a risk makes no sense. The way I feel about it is not good. If I can't be comfortable making decisions, I need to get out.

"I told Dominic and Connie that George is a friend and that I wanted them to evaluate their feelings about how much of a risk he was to us. If they felt uncomfortable, the door was open to eliminating him, but if not to call me and we would work out a solution to the problem. You two know George so well I didn't know if you'd be comfortable doing this. Maybe I was wrong; you're professionals, and it might have been better if you two explained things to him and did the job. But what's done is done. They'll call us when it's taken care of. All we can do is wait."

Worn out, emotionally and physically, George skipped the final session. He took an early shuttle to the airport only to learn his flight had been canceled. The attendant at the customer service counter was able, due to his early arrival, to get him on a flight to Hartford but there were no first-class seats available.

He raced through the airport and arrived at his departure gate just in time. The change in flights left him with an aisle seat in coach. He settled down and, before pulling his New York Yankees cap down over his eyes, noted the other two passengers in his row and thanked God the big guy was in the window seat and the little lady was in the middle. George knew enough to avoid all eye contact when sitting next to a woman, if you wanted peace and quiet. His fears were well grounded.

The big guy had his head on a pillow, snoring. His seat mate finished stowing her bag and turned to him. "I was trying to get to New York, but my flight was canceled. How about you?"

George mumbled an answer, showing no interest in being sociable but this didn't stop her.

"It's exhausting to sit in airports and wait on lines. I was lucky to get on this flight. I have to get to New York for a meeting. I hope I can rent a car. Where are you going when we land?"

"Someone is meeting me. I live in Connecticut. Same distance to either airport." George tried to end their discussion by pulling the cap even further down over his eyes. He envied the big guy. He couldn't turn away because he was on the aisle.

"I live in Orlando. What brought you down?"

"I had a meeting." George was beginning to get annoyed and tilted his seat back.

"What kind of business are you in? What do you do?"

George knew the answer was the key to his serenity. If he told her he was a surgeon he'd get no rest; she'd ply him for free medical advice. He needed an occupation that would silence her. A lawyer? Mortician, maybe? No, she might be a necrophiliac or something. What is it that a woman wouldn't want to talk about? Ah, a urologist! That ought to cool their exchange. She wouldn't want to discuss bladder dysfunction with a stranger, even if he were a doctor.

George sat up, looked down at her, and said in a deep, masculine voice: "I'm a urologist."

"So am I! I'm going to New York for the American College of Urology meeting."

George burst out laughing so loudly that all the passengers craned their heads. His seat mate wanted to know what was so funny.

Once he was able to stop laughing, he told her the truth and she had a good laugh, too. The remainder of the flight was fun for George and his urologist friend. They shared stories; George told her about both of his head injuries and their repercussions, feeling perfectly safe, knowing they would not meet again. It was a beneficial and healing flight on Therapeutic Airlines.

The crazy coincidence energized George. He wondered how God had the time to work out all these details like foul balls and seat mates. Amazing. His mother always talked about God's redirections, but he didn't buy it as a teenager. Maybe his mother knew something about the universe's schedule—how we created our future unconsciously and there really were no coincidences.

He would have had even more faith in his mother's wisdom if he had known what the change in his flight had done for him. He called Carmine on his cell from the plane to report the change.

"Gabriel, glad I caught you. My flight was canceled. I'm coming into Bradley. I can get home on my own, but you need to tell the limo not to wait. I also have a favor to ask for a friend who needs a ride into New York."

"Hang on, George, let me tell Carmine."

"Boss, it's George. His flight was canceled, and he's headed for Hartford with a friend who needs a ride. What do you want to do?"

Carmine burst out laughing. "He falls off a ladder, gets hit in the head, has his flight canceled, and comes out smelling like a rose. Every time he says, 'Oh, shit,' he's rescued. He must have a guardian angel by that name. Tell him you'll meet him at Bradley and to wait for you in the restaurant. Gentlemen, it's back in our hands."

Gabriel passed Carmine's message on to George.

If George had known who was waiting at LaGuardia, he would have stopped doubting his mother entirely. Bubbles, Cookie, Dominic, and Connie were all there. Bubbles and Cookie notified airport security of their presence and intentions. Being early, they headed for the lounge near the security area where the arriving passengers would exit.

When Dominic and Connie arrived the only lounge seats available were at a table where two well-dressed men looking like businessmen sat, probably waiting for their flight. One man was lanky, the other much shorter and rather fidgety.

"Mind if we join you?" said Dominic. "We're picking up a friend."

The little guy answered. "No problem."

"Dominic and Connie."

"Sam and Marv."

"Thanks for sharing the table. Can we buy you a drink?"

"No, thanks. We're fine."

"You guys off on a business trip?"

"No, meeting someone too."

"Connie, what's the flight number of George's plane?" Connie told him. "I'll check the screen to see if it's on time."

In their excitement Bubbles and Cookie hadn't thought much about what arrangements George had made about getting home. There was a noticeable change in the conversation as each looked at the other knowingly. Cookie excused himself to use the men's room, notified security and told them to hold all passengers on the plane. He and Bubbles would board the plane, take George into custody, and lead him down the ramp stairs to a car waiting on the tarmac.

Dominic returned with his report. "It says canceled on a bunch of flights, including his."

Just then an announcement explained the cancellations were due to a runway closure. Bubbles and Cookie had learned, from the passenger list that George was on his way to Hartford. It was too late to drive up and meet his plane, so they decided to stake out his house.

Dominic and Constantine sensed a change in their tablemates following the mention of George's name. They called Carmine on the drive back to share their suspicions. Carmine told them to cancel their previous arrangement and await further instructions.

When George's flight landed, Michael and Gabriel were waiting. George's seat mate Linda, was impressed by the welcoming committee. Upon arriving at Carmine's house, Michael led the doctor to a limo. She thanked them all and gave them her card. "In case any of you ever need prostate surgery."

George went straight to the den. The door was open. Carmine was going over some papers with two men.

"Am I interrupting you?"

"No, come in, we're just about done. Patrick, Jason, I find this quite acceptable. Our misunderstandings are a thing of the past. I'll see that the right people are informed." They shook hands, embraced, and departed, walking past George as if he didn't exist.

"I hear you made a new friend on your flight, George," said Carmine.

"Never mind that, Carmine. I'm exhausted. Can I get right to the point? I need to talk about our past relationship and plans. I feel like I'm going to explode if I don't get a chance to talk."

"I can appreciate that. Go ahead." Carmine felt no pressure. He had all his options open and was directing the movie.

George took a deep breath. "I've had full recall of our plans for that weekend in Vermont and told my wife everything. I came here for two reasons. One, I never had any intention to place my wife at risk but was using her to get you to open up and to convince you to change your mind about your wife, if that was your intention. Second, and perhaps of greater importance, I want to assure you I will never ever say anything to anyone that may incriminate you. I am grateful to you for what you've done for me and my family. You had options and gave me a chance, for whatever reasons. Speaking from my heart, I know there is another side to you. I've seen you as a friend and grandfather, and that's the man I will protect.

"I can't predict your reaction; I can only live the truth with you. I'll go home now, if you have faith in me, to see where my marriage stands. I have asked Honey to give our marriage another chance. What I've been through has taught me a great deal, and I believe I can deal with my problems. I hope to convince you to think about your relationship too. Life is a riddle; we need solutions that don't hurt anyone. I think we can eliminate the things that bother us and not the person or the relationship."

Carmine reared back in his chair, took a drag on his expensive cigar, and blew a perfect smoke ring.

"To come here and say what you did took guts. I also thank you for believing in me—or at least in that part of me that touched you. What you fantasize is your problem. I never had any intention of eliminating Maria or Honey. You were a sick man to think that because I wanted to involve my wife in some way, it meant I wanted to kill her.

"While you were busy trying to manipulate me, I was recording what you said to use it to pressure you into helping with a business deal. Remember, I have the recording and I won't make any promises, but I'll take your words seriously. If you have no objection, I'll go home with you and have a few words with Honey. Then I'll make my decision while the two of you try to work things out.

"You seem to live a charmed life, George, even if it doesn't look that way to you. Your life has become so entertaining that it seems inappropriate to conclude it prematurely. I'll give you a little time and see what develops."

"I'll agree to help you in any way, legal or not," said George. "I know this is asking a lot of you and I don't have many options. I'll call Honey and tell her we're on our way."

The ride to George's house was silent but comfortable. George was at peace with himself and Carmine knew he was acting out of faith. He felt like family.

Michael remained in the limo as George, Carmine, and Gabriel went inside. A few minutes later, Seltzer and Graham pulled up behind the limo. Michael recognized them from the description Dominic had given on the phone. Michael stole around to the kitchen door as the lawmen walked up to the front door and rang the bell.

"I'll get it." George opened the door while Honey and Carmine sat in the kitchen talking.

Identifying themselves and flashing their credentials, the dynamic duo elbowed their way inside. "George Dingfelder," said Graham, sounding most Cagney-esque, "you are under arrest for conspiracy to commit murder."

George was handcuffed and read his rights.

He was totally stunned. "What the hell is going on here? I've told you a million times that—"

"We have a recording of your recent phone conversations," said Graham. "It would be best if you just came along quietly now."

"You guys must be nuts. If you listened to the tape you know my thoughts and plans don't threaten anyone. I'm here with my wife. What the hell are you talking about?"

Carmine and Honey came out of the kitchen, with Gabriel and Michael looming menacingly behind them. The appearance of the racketeer and his hulking associates silenced even the garrulous Graham.

Meanwhile the kids, responding to the commotion, had come out of their rooms. They stared bewilderedly at the sight of their father in handcuffs.

Carmine looked at the lawmen with disdain. "Well, well, well, if it ain't Bubbles and Cookie, the Abbott and Costello of law enforcement. You clowns can't get to me, so you go after Dingfelder. He offers me his assistance, has marital problems, and you make him a criminal. You ought to be ashamed of the way you waste taxpayers' money. If you want me, come and get me! Leave this poor guy alone. He's not a criminal and you damn well know it. You can't scare him into lying about me."

George stepped between them. "I'm no idiot. I know what you want but if you think threatening me is going to get me to incriminate Mr. Birsamatto, you're crazy. This man was like a father to me while I struggled to regain my health and memory. He's here to help me and my wife. Did you jerks notice he was in the kitchen talking to my wife and not in the living room with me hatching a sinister plot?"

Honey was incensed by this latest insane development. "You idiots, release my husband and get out of here! He may be mentally defective but he's seeing a psychiatrist and he's no criminal. I'll never press charges! If you thought he was a threat why didn't you call me and tell me, or offer me protection? You know damn well this is ludicrous; it's just what Mr. Birsamatto said it was: a setup. You're not interested in protecting me, just incriminating these men. Well, it won't work. If you had really listened to our phone calls you would know he's no threat and we're here to straighten out our marriage. Is either one of you married? Stop this idiotic behavior!"

Seltzer and Graham remained silent. They couldn't argue with her logic, but they had their job to do. They had come this far and were reluctant to give up their pursuit of Carmine too easily. Honey's shouting as he was led away attracted the neighbors' attention; a knot of spectators, including Charlie Pomeroy, assembled on the sidewalk. Carmine tried to calm her. Michael and Gabriel waited for a sign from Carmine to intervene. He shook his head no.

"George, I'll get you an attorney as soon as I can," said Carmine. "It's clear this is about getting to me so just keep your mouth shut until my attorney arrives."

George didn't have time to answer as the lawmen pushed him roughly into the back seat of the car and drove off. Carmine put his arm around Honey, and they went back into the house. He phoned his attorney, Steve Geiger, reassured Honey and talked to the children. Carmine had a way with kids.

He drove back to Fairfield and called his associates to let them know of the developments and his decision regarding George. He explained they had more to fear if George felt he or his family was threatened.

George was held overnight. The following day, Judge Dunklee presided at his arraignment hearing. Gabriel, Honey, Eunice, and the children all attended. Carmine, preferring to stay out of the limelight, did not appear. The state's case was presented. When they were finished Geiger, George's attorney, rose to speak. Dunklee interrupted him.

"Excuse me, Mr. Geiger, but let me see if I can save us all some time and aggravation. This case is unique—bizarre psychologically as well as legally. I am aware that Mr. Dingfelder has had a brain injury and previous psychotherapy. And I have learned from experience that at times eminently reasonable and totally logical decisions are completely wrong. I do not see any case against your client at this time, but I need to be sure he is stable emotionally before I release him. Therefore, I plan to follow my gut feelings. If the state's attorney and your client agree to his confinement to an in-patient psychiatric facility for evaluation of his competency, I will waive bail, with the stipulation that

Mr. Dingfelder wear an ankle bracelet and not leave the facility, for any reason, without court permission."

All heads nodded in agreement after a short consultation.

"So be it. I will see that arrangements are made, and we will reconvene when his evaluation is completed. Court's adjourned."

Carmine was pleased by the distraction and confusion George was causing Seltzer and Graham. He instructed Geiger to tell George he would stop by and visit when business allowed. He explained to his associates that George could be trusted. He was one of them now, and they needn't feel threatened by the tenuous case against George. He didn't discuss the fact that George's problem had become a therapeutic distraction—more like a Hitchcock mystery than a Woody Allen comedy.

No one objected to Dunklee's decision, made after consulting with Hokmah, to have George admitted to Peaceful Acres in Middlefield.

CHAPTER 18

After evaluating George, it was clear to Hokmah that he was not a threat to anyone, but there was still the possibility that he could revert to fantasizing once out in the real world. Carmine was smart enough to remain his patient, knowing he was protected by physician-patient privilege, as long as he was not a direct threat to anyone.

Hokmah did not discuss his regression experience with George but did introduce guided imagery into their therapy sessions at George's request, since he had a positive experience in this area at the medical meeting in Florida. He also consented to some of George's sessions taking place while they jogged cross-country. He questioned the benefit of this until the day George suddenly stopped running during a discussion about his wives.

"Remember that tree that grew around the barbed wire. Great role model. I just wish I could deal with all the barbed wire in my life the way that tree has.

"Sometimes I wonder: what's the point of all this is? Why go on? What are we here for? God didn't do a good job if you ask me. Or maybe God is just an underachiever."

"George, we've been asking 'Why me?' since the time of Job. When you find the answer, you'll understand the nature of life. If you were God, you'd understand why. Understanding doesn't eliminate life's difficulties, but when your afflictions have meaning you stop suffering. This reminds me of a joke."

"I could use a good laugh," said George.

"Okay. What is the most frequent question in heaven and on earth?" George shrugged. "On earth it's 'Where's the bathroom,' and in Heaven it's 'Why was I so serious back there?'"

"Good one, Jon. But don't quit your day job."

Hokmah turned into the cemetery they were passing. "Maybe we should just leave a reading list to help people become enlightened and a note on our headstone that says, 'See you all later, just getting some rest.'"

They were laughing over ideas for their epitaphs when they came upon James Earnest Cooper's headstone. Chiseled into it were the dates he went to Yale and Harvard law school, a paragraph about his forty-year business career as a lawyer and manufacturer in Connecticut, and the dates of his birth and death.

"Look, he died forty-one years after graduation from law school."

"So, what are you saying George?"

"He retired and died. No work, no reason to go on living. Sad. His wife outlived him by decades, and she doesn't list her college degrees. I'm beginning to realize the significance of relationships and a meaningful life."

"Yes, George, we need to live authentic lives and not roles. Then you don't have to die when you retire, or the kids leave home. It's important to burn up, not out."

"Jon, how do you think Cooper introduced himself to God? Yale lawyer? Harvard lawyer? Manufacturer? I wonder if God was impressed or told him to come back when he knew who he was."

"Yeah, reminds me when God asked Adam, 'Where are you?' I think He was talking about his presence in life and not his physical location. Though I have to add, if he were a New York lawyer they'd probably have let him in, because he was probably the first New York lawyer God ever met."

When they got back to Peaceful Acres, Carmine's limo had just pulled up.

"Did you guys ever stop to think what would happen if you used the same skills in your relationships as you do in business or with your kids and animals?"

"Jon it's not the same thing. In business I have a relationship that is carefully defined. George's dogs may require attention and training but they're probably less trouble than a wife. If I have a business problem, I meet the person face to face. You talked about this woman shrink you met; maybe she and our wives should join us."

"Yes, Carmine relationships are work. I was hoping you'd see that. We all have to realize that a perfect world is not creation and would make our lives meaningless."

Hokmah was happy to get the dialogue and group sessions started. He was impressed by what the three couples were able to accomplish. At times not only the wives but also the children and grandchildren joined them. The freedom to speak their feelings and the different sexes, ages, and generations had a profound effect upon them all. As he had learned, when in doubt behave and act as if you were the person you want to be and keep rehearsing until you get it right.

The children kept everyone grounded in the present and when they suggested family competitive relay jogging, Hokmah realized there was more to therapy than talking. Creating teams opened the door to talking in an unguarded way, and he was no longer sure who the group leader was at times.

On their next jogging session George turned to Hokmah and said, "I was afraid to tell you, but I keep hearing voices. The words are generally helpful, but God knows where they're coming from."

"You could be psychotic, but I think you're finally ready to listen to your unconscious."

Carmine added, "It's more likely you're out of your mind."

When Dunklee's office called to obtain the final evaluation of George's competency, Hokmah responded, "I'll have it completed right after our fall picnic, Your Honor. Why don't you, Graham, and Seltzer come and observe George and Carmine for yourselves, as well as just enjoy the festivities? In addition to my report, seeing them and their families interact should help in your final decision."

CHAPTER 19

One evening, while reaching into the pocket of the jacket he had worn on the flight home from the medical conference, Hokmah rediscovered Judy's note.

"Why did you put this in my luggage?"

"Because I know you have your hands full Jon, but I want our marriage to work, and I know you do too, but changing jobs hasn't made your work less stressful. You need to focus on our family and be aware of our needs, just as you do your patients' needs. We need to function as a team and make things easier for us all. You are not responsible for everyone and everything."

"At least I've never fantasized eliminating my problems—starting with my wife—like George."

"That's not funny! It works both ways. Women are capable of eliminating or castrating husbands. You read the papers, so stay alert and awake. What Honey experienced is no joke."

"I'm sorry, that was in bad taste. I didn't mean to minimize the problem. Believe me, I care about you."

———※———

The wives were happy to work on their own issues with a female therapist like Inge, and have the women outnumber the men. It gave them a sense of family and the power to make a difference. Inge was impressed by the women's desire to build relationships. She realized they had done a great deal of work prior to her coming but couldn't understand their equanimity.

While sitting in a group session with the women Inge said to Honey, "I don't know how you can sit here discussing your husband as if all he did was come home late from work. Why aren't you expressing appropriate anger? Being polite is one thing, but being a submissive martyr is not survival behavior. Saying no and asking for help are survival characteristics."

"Inge, I've made plenty of noise but at some point, you realize you've screamed it all out and haven't solved anything. All you're left with is an emptiness that doesn't feel good either. I'm looking for ways to fill the void and nourish myself and my life.

"I want to find a way to heal. As long as my health and well-being are not threatened, I'll keep trying to heal things with love as long as my husband does. Divorce and castration are still options but, if we decide to go that route, it will be for the right reasons and not out of rage. You came too late to see the stuff psychiatrists enjoy. I want to be a love warrior. Yes, love is my weapon."

"Right on, Honey," Inge replied.

"Inge, are you here to criticize or guide us? If we're unusual, so be it and accept it and us."

"I'm with you Maria. My criticism is meant to guide you and the group, like a coach, and get you to react and improve, not to put you down."

"Inge I'd like you to know that my husband does understand and appreciate my willingness to forgive," Honey responded. "Men seem to be of another species. I don't know how their brains are wired but I think we have to listen to their reasons for behaving the way they do and learn to understand them."

"I agree. When love is involved, aggression finds healthy ways to be expressed. When we can admit the desire to murder, rather than project it onto others, it brings it out of the shadow. When one consciously accepts that fact it can be dealt with and is less likely to happen. I don't know if it would help the men understand or how they would react if their lives were threatened by you. I certainly cannot recommend it as a therapeutic tool."

Inge did not notice the sparkle in Maria's eye when she finished. Maria winked and gave Honey a knowing nod. The group therapy was empowering the women and they felt the change.

When the session ended, Maria took Honey aside. "Remember the punch line: Never argue with a woman when she is tired…or rested. And: Never go to bed mad…stay up and fight. We're going to do a therapeutic poisoning of our husbands to help them understand. Carmine's been very quiet lately and just won't talk. I can't tell what's on his mind. My idea may get him talking again."

"How can you say a thing like that? I refuse to be a part of anything that is going to hurt anyone."

"Listen a minute. When I was in college my sorority sisters put Ex-Lax in the chocolate icing of a cake we made for our fraternity brothers to get even with them for something they did. It was a blast for all the sorority sisters, not to mention what it did to the frat house. We caught hell from our faculty advisor, but it was worth it.

"Here's my plan. You and George come over for dinner. I'll make sure the four of us are alone. You and I will prepare the meal. We "poison" the dessert and make them suspicious of our intentions when the poison begins to take effect. They'll have some idea of your thoughts and feelings after that."

"How are you going to figure out what to give them? You're no doctor."

"I'm sure Inge may have some suggestions. After all, women have to stick together. We can tell her the sorority story and that someone we know wants to do the same thing. We don't have to tell her the truth."

At their next group session Inge couldn't help laughing when Honey and Maria broached their scheme. "I'd suggest cascara, which causes diarrhea. And don't mention my name. I don't want to be sued for malpractice and I don't want to hear what happens. Just be sure that you follow directions and don't overdose them."

Before she left the session, Hokmah spoke to Inge. "I'm ready to share my experience with George and Carmine and utilize regression therapy if they agree. Please discuss it with the women and see if they want to participate."

———※———

The following Saturday, Honey and George arrived at Carmine's for dinner. The entire staff, including Michael and Gabriel, was given the night off.

Maria welcomed everyone, "Let's all relax and be ourselves for one evening."

Carmine raised his glass. "A toast to the future and our loved ones."

George added, "And to everyone's health and well-being."

Maria and Honey had a hard time stifling their giggles while sipping the wine. George and Carmine wondered what the women thought was so funny. The meal was elegant Italian cuisine. George and Carmine were impressed by their wives' culinary skills. They could hear the laughter coming from the kitchen before each course.

"They certainly seem to be getting along well and are a lot more relaxed," George observed. "Their sessions with Inge must be making a difference."

George agreed. "Maria has been a good influence too. Honey has cut way down on her smoking and is taking long walks with some of the women in our neighborhood."

After a leisurely meal and small talk, dessert was served in the sunroom: a delectable chocolate mousse with an Oreo cookie crust, accompanied by a foaming cup of cafe latte.

"Guys just relax and enjoy your dessert. No calorie counting tonight. It's low-fat, we promise. We couldn't resist having our dessert in the kitchen while we were getting things ready. So, enjoy yourselves. Honey and I will clean up and join you for coffee."

When they finished serving, Honey and Maria cleared the table, sat down, sipped their lattes, and waited.

"How's everything? Are we good cooks or what? Finish everything on your plate or we'll think you don't love us. Here, have seconds."

"Thanks Maria, who can resist chocolate. What's got you two so energized? All night you've been going a mile a minute."

"Nothing special George. Just having a good time and happy to please. Would you like another serving? You only live once. Remember that wise old saying: 'Life is uncertain; eat dessert first.'"

George noticed feelings of queasiness and bowel urgency but didn't want to spoil the evening, until it became impossible to ignore.

"I'm feeling a little full. Maybe I ate too much or have a virus."

"I didn't want to say anything, but I don't feel well either. Maria, are you sure the food was fresh?"

"Carmine, you know I only buy organic foods." She looked at Honey. "How do you feel?"

"I feel fine."

"Me too. Shall I check the medicine chest and bring something for you boys?

"Please!" George and Carmine chorused.

"All right. Come on, Honey, let's go find something. Be right back, boys."

When the women left, Carmine looked at George. "Do you think they would...?"

"Would what?"

"Do you think Honey would do anything, well, crazy?"

"Carmine, what are you suggesting?" George's churning bowels made a sound like two dragons copulating. "Oh God, I need to get to the bathroom!"

George ran down the hall towards the guest bathroom, fighting to maintain control of his GI tract. He lost the battle in the hallway.

Honey and Maria returned.

"Wonder what his problem is? Couldn't be the food," said Honey.

Maria concurred. "Right, we all had the same thing. Is he lactose intolerant, Honey?"

"Not that I'm aware of. Maybe he just ate too much."

Carmine said, "What about medication? Don't we have any Pepto-Bismol or something?"

"No, I'm afraid not," said Maria with an evil gleam in her eye. "You don't look so good, either darling. You're positively green! How do you feel?"

"I'll tell you how I feel. I feel like I'm about to… oh, *shit!*"

"He's got that right," deadpanned Honey, as Carmine raced to the maid's bathroom.

He could hear George in the guest bathroom while he performed in the maid's room. The unholy sounds emanating from their gastrointestinal tracts reverberated throughout the house.

The two sorority sisters felt sorry for what they had done—for about thirty seconds—and then were laughing so hard tears were running down their cheeks. When their pale, disheveled spouses returned, they couldn't help bursting out laughing again.

"What the hell is so funny?" Carmine demanded. "You two obviously feel fine, so what's going on? Did you put something in the dessert? Maria, did you? Honey? So that's why the two of you ate your dessert in the kitchen! After all we've…"

The sentence remained unfinished as off he went for a second session of gastrointestinal cleansing. George was right behind him.

Finally, when their exhausted hubbies could sit still, Maria addressed them. "You're right; we contaminated your dessert, or to say it in a nicer way, we overdosed you with cascara to get you to appreciate what Honey had to deal with. Maybe we were a wee bit cruel but now we're a little closer to understanding each other's experience. Here's a big hug, a bathrobe, and some bottled water. Somehow, I don't think you want us to serve you anything more to eat. Don't worry, we didn't spike the water too."

"Oh, I wouldn't be too sure of that," Honey added mischievously.

It was all Maria and Honey could do to keep from bursting out laughing again as they looked at their two depleted mates staring vacantly into space, wondering whether they knew the women they were married to anymore.

The evening turned out to be a success when a bottle of fine wine helped Carmine's sense of humor return. He complimented Maria: "If anyone ever needs a female hit man, you can count on my recommendation."

CHAPTER 20

Hokmah started his next session with George and Carmine with some news. "Before we begin, I want you to know I invited Seltzer, Graham, Dunklee, and Newman to our picnic. Thank God, Dunklee is a reasonable guy and has kept the others under control. It seems the three of us have acquired quite a reputation in medical, judicial, and law enforcement circles. I think they all plan to attend.

"They are professionals doing their jobs, but I want them to see us as people and not criminal cases. We all need to have a heart not just a brain. Many schools are named Sacred Heart Academy but none I know of as Sacred Brain.

"Next, I'd like to share an experience with you. While in San Francisco I participated in a workshop on past lives and regression therapy, which I previously had no interest or belief in, but despite my negativity it affected me deeply."

"How so?" George asked.

"I believe my past life experience reveals a lot about the choices I decided to make in this life, including my need to become a psychiatrist and to heal wounds with words. This is still not easy for me to talk about. In fact, besides my wife and Inge, you two are the only ones I have discussed this with."

"What does this have to do with us?" Carmine asked.

"I think it helps to explain why I'm living this life. If my pain can educate me, I can help others turn from self-destructive behavior to life-enhancing behavior and save a lot of lives.

"For the first time I understood I shaved my head to uncover feelings and to foster spirituality, like the ritual shaving monks do. So here I am, learning more in one brief regression session than from all those years of psychiatric training and analysis. My life isn't a puzzle anymore and I feel more at peace. The only person I have problems with now is me."

Carmine shifted restlessly in his seat. "You keep yammering on and on, Jon. Cut to the chase. What's in it for *me*?"

"Just this, Carmine: I think you will find understanding too. From your expression I suppose you feel I'm out of my mind. Whether you believe or not is unimportant. What you experience is what matters."

George, his liquid eyes wide open, unblinking, was mesmerized by the subject. Carmine remained skeptical.

"Why do something that doesn't make sense?" the racketeer grumbled. "When people die, they die. You're telling me something lives on. I find that hard to believe. If it's true, then why don't all those spirits get together and get even with the people who treated them like shit during their lifetime? Or are they just waiting for me to show up in spirit land?"

Carmine saw concern, not judgment, in their eyes. He went on:

"Ah, it makes no sense. And here's another question. I've heard about near-death and out-of-body experiences, and people whose spirits come back five years later and save someone's life. What the hell have they been doing for five years? Why waste time? Why aren't they back in a new body going to school or saving the world? And who decides who you come back as, and where and when, for that matter? Do you apply for the position? With all this going on, where does God fit in—if there even is a God? I even heard someone say time

182

ceases to exist when you leave your body. Come on, none of it makes any sense. It's a bunch of metaphysical hooey."

"Look I don't have all the answers," said Hokmah. "They do say when you leave your body there is only energy and consciousness. The mystics, quantum physicists, and astronomers understand it better than I do. I'm no Einstein, and I don't know if we will ever understand it. We and all life are a wonderful mystery too.

"I have questions too, but I also have my experience. That is what I want to offer you gentlemen: experience. The question is: do you want to give it a try? Your experience might alter your beliefs. If it helps you get your life in order and understand why you decided to be like your grandfather, or why your grandson is HIV positive, what difference does it make? What we're after are answers and change. If you can accept the experience and let it help you the explanation is of secondary importance. Let the intellectuals and scientists work on it. After you have the experience you won't need explanations.

"Doctors are always writing books when what they didn't believe in suddenly happens to them. You'll believe because of the result. Its effectiveness I can vouch for. Whether past lives are real or not doesn't matter. I can't explain how past consciousness impregnates our brains but that doesn't matter. The other day I saw a human-interest feature on the news about a five-year-old violin virtuoso playing with a concert orchestra. How did he become so talented? Why a violin? How did some people become HIV negative before treatment was available or others have their cancers heal? The result is what counts, not trying to explain the unexplainable.

"Think of it this way, if consciousness is trying to become matter to create life, maybe matter needs to become conscious in order to participate in creation. Maybe we are God's tools; when our bodies die, God recycles our energy and consciousness and love to make it easier for those who come after us. Life is a circle and it never ends.

"Will you join me on this journey? What do you say, gents?"

George's intellectually oriented way of thinking was in total disorder. "I'll go!" he said emphatically because something deep inside him felt Jon was speaking the truth.

Carmine smiled. "What the hell do I have to lose? We've come a long way together. So, what the hell. Maybe life is a school. You work your way up through the grades and get educated by your experience."

Hokmah was pleased with their responses and ready to begin. "I'm going to play a CD I picked up at the conference by noted regression therapist, Dr. Brian Weiss. Just listen and let the voice go with you. When you're ready, look up and let your eyes close gently. Remember, God speaks in dreams and images."

He started the CD and Weiss began speaking: "My voice will go with you. You are free to follow my voice or not, but it will go with you on the journey you are about to take. You will be in complete control. There is nothing to fear.

"This journey will take you back in time. You will grow younger and return to a time prior to your birth, where you will become one with the sights, sounds, feelings, and all the senses you experience. Guides may appear to assist you on your journey.

"You will continue past the time of your birth and remain aware of the surroundings, people, and sights you encounter. Do not think, for you are not ready for thought, as you return to the time and place that feels right for you. When you arrive, the place will feel familiar. For whatever reason you have come to this place and time, let yourself experience what you need to relive, and learn and understand why you are living this life."

George questioned whether anything could explain his feelings or crazy interests. Were they coincidences or not? His confusion and desire to know deepened his trance.

Carmine had no objection to trying to learn something helpful and cooperating, even if it only helped George. If he benefited, too, so much the better. He didn't see how a past life could help him to understand his present one. Sure, what he had done in this life affected him, but what difference could what he did in a past life make, if he even had one? He was smiling to himself at how crazy it all was. He felt like a kid with a new toy and was glad Michael and Gabriel weren't there. He wouldn't want word to get out about this cockamamie business. Maybe some great dignitary would show up to guide him; that would be a hoot to talk about.

As Weiss's mellifluous voice continued its hypnotic dialogue, images began to appear which had a life of their own.

George initially felt as if he were in a theater watching a play or a movie. A group of exhausted men, carrying bloody weapons, were riding on horseback towards a castle. As they reached the castle the gate was raised, and they rode on into the courtyard. George was no longer watching but living the experience as he entered a large dining hall and, genuflecting to his lord, informed him of the battle's victorious outcome. When he finished, his lord bade him rise. They went down the hall to a high-ceilinged room illuminated by a fire.

"Ebba, I know you are tired but there is something I need to discuss with you. Our neighboring lord does not respect our boundaries, nor does he listen to reason. It is time for us to teach him a lesson. I want you to slay his daughter so that he is aware of my feelings and respects my rights and property."

"My lord, might there not be another way to solve the problem? Perhaps killing her father and sparing her life?"

"Do you not have faith in my decision and judgment? It is either her life or yours. Which shall it be? You call me your lord and yet do not have faith in your lord. How can this be? You either take her life or I will take yours. Decide now."

"I shall not question your choice, though I have always questioned Abraham and Jesus and their faith regarding what their Lord asked of them. I shall explore how I may best carry out your wishes."

The following day Ebba, despite his misgivings regarding his lord's request, rode to a place in the forest from which he could view the neighboring castle. Upon his return he said:

"My lord, I have seen the young woman and will speak from my heart. If I must kill someone, I say again: why not kill her father?"

"Ebba, it is your choice. I am tired of talking about it. Her life or yours, which shall it be?"

Neither faith nor courage were involved in Ebba's decision. He could not understand his lord's decision but feared for his life.

"I shall carry out your wish. I only ask that you give me time to find a way that will cause the least suffering for the young woman."

"So be it."

Ebba rode to the castle the following day.

"I am a weary traveler looking for a place to rest," Ebba said to the gatekeeper. "I would be happy to work in return for food and shelter."

Because of his shabby attire and diffident manner, the gatekeeper deemed Ebba harmless. Ebba was admitted to the castle and provided with a place to stay, with the freedom to explore the castle without arousing suspicion. He learned where his victim's room was but avoided any contact with her. He knew he could choose to desert his lord and not carry out his order, but he feared the dire consequences.

Late the following evening he climbed the long stone staircase that led to her room; drawing his sword, he opened the door and stepped inside. Her dog arose, growling menacingly. Ebba brought the sword down on his skull. The dull thud of the impact, the gushing blood, and the dying animal's pitiful whimpering sickened George.

In the midst of this vision, George recalled reading the story "Wolfen" to his son Carl about a knight who returns from the war and upon entering his newborn son's room finds an overturned crib and his dog covered with blood. Thinking his dog has killed his son, he draws his sword and kills the animal. When he rights the crib, he finds a dead wolf and his son, unharmed. His beloved dog had saved his child's life and the knight, in his blind anger, had killed him. Carl, who was very young at the time and didn't quite appreciate the moral, had said, "Dad, it's only a story." But it was more than a story. George now understood and welcomed the sobs that shook his body. His mind was a storehouse of timeless images and feelings. He felt healed and cleansed as his tears washed away his guilt. He understood his need to rescue and care for dogs since his childhood.

Before Ebba could reach the young woman, the sounds of the dying dog awakened her. She turned. It was Honey. Ebba severed her neck with one stroke of his sword. Honey's head lay at his feet, her sightless eyes staring up at him.

Ebba returned to the castle and dropped the bloody head at his lord's feet.

"I hope my lord is pleased."

"Ebba, you made the choice and performed the act. Had you had faith in me, said yes, and not questioned my judgment, you would have had a different experience. But because you did not have faith in me, a needless death occurred. Fear is your Lord, not I. Jesus and Abraham had faith in their Lord. They didn't bargain or make excuses. They had faith, and their Lord could trust and believe in them. You cannot be trusted. If I could have trusted you, because of your faith in me, none of this would have happened."

At the same time Carmine sat smiling to himself in anticipation of what great man he had been in a past life. He fully expected Moses, Jesus, Buddha, or someone of equal stature to appear. When no great dignitary appeared, his thinking stopped, and spontaneous images began to appear.

A large clearing appeared, set back from the ocean, filled with tents, horses, campfires, men and women working, and children playing on the beach.

He was among a group of teenagers, playing the part of the tribe's warriors and hunters, searching for a boy who was hiding in the beach grass. When they found him, they acted out killing him with driftwood spears. They then lifted him onto their shoulders and carried him back to the village in triumph.

He saw his mother waving to him. "Juaquin, I need your help."

As he responded to his mother's call a group of men on horseback charged into the clearing, killing all those before them except for the young women. Juaquin watched his family die and his sisters being carried off. The boys tried to hide in the beach grass, but a group of horsemen saw them and rode them down. He screamed when the sword struck his back.

When the horsemen rode off, he pulled himself back to camp with his arms. His body was numb, a useless weight trailing blood. He chanted the tribal death ritual and covered his family's bodies as best he could. His rage kept him alive. He prayed to his gods to help him avenge his family. Why did the gods let this happen? He couldn't understand why they didn't create a world free of wars and evil.

He lay down next to his parents recalling their shaman's words: "Your body is impermanent. You are here to learn to love and achieve wisdom which your spirit will carry forward so that when you are born again and again, on the wheel of rebirth, you may use it for the benefit of others."

Juaquin shouted, "Never again will I let this happen! I shall be the one who is feared. No one will ever hurt my family again. I will protect them and avenge any injury done to them. I swear it."

Juaquin's vow to be like the people he despised felt like a knife penetrating Carmine's heart. As Weiss's voice brought them back to a state of awareness and conscious of the present, Carmine became aware of George sobbing in the seat next to him and Jon's words helping them gently return to the room.

What the hell had Hokmah done? How was this supposed to help? It reminded him of a horror movie. He didn't appreciate it at all.

"I know how emotional this can be," said Jon. "The best thing for us all is to take a moment and not say anything. Just do some deep breathing for a few minutes. If you need to cry, don't be ashamed; express your feelings freely."

Carmine and George were so drained they closed their eyes again.

As their emotional response subsided, Hokmah spoke: "I'd like you to live with your experience for a day. Do not discuss it with anyone but carry on with the person or persons you met in the regression. Let them and tonight's dreams be your guides and therapists. Tomorrow we will discuss your experience and what you feel you have learned from this, and how that experience has made you the man you are today."

George and Carmine were too numb to answer. Hokmah took their silence for a sign of agreement.

"I apologize for the emotional pain this may have caused. Believe me, what you have learned and will learn will help you for the rest of your lives. And the pain, like a labor pain, will lead to the birth of your true self and be well worth the price."

He embraced them both before they parted.

CHAPTER 21

The following day, three somber musketeers met.

Jon asked, "Do you guys need a relaxation exercise before we begin?"

"Shit, Jon, enough already!" said Carmine. "You asked me to live with this and I did. I don't plan to play a CD every time I have a problem. Yesterday's experience led me to a new understanding of my life. I'm no therapist, but I do have something to say. And if my words don't make sense, we still have your bullshit."

"Carmine, the floor is yours. Let me say I didn't do it *to* you or *for* you. I can coach you, but I can't change you. You had to have the desire and intention. Ready whenever you are. So, let's begin to share our past life stories."

After their unique stories were shared in detail, George interrupted their discussion, "Wait one minute! I can't sit here without asking something. Did the past really happen? Is it something I really did? It felt real, but was it? Is it my imagination or like a dream which helps you, but isn't your real life?"

"George, I feel it is true that our consciousness exists after our body dies," said Jon, "and that those who are born after us are impregnated with our consciousness and experiences. But as a scientist, I'm also a skeptic. Read Weiss's books and you'll see he was skeptical, too, until his patients' experiences made him a believer.

"I can't tell you who or what decides what consciousness comes with you and how you come back or what you are here to learn. Carmine raised those questions yesterday. Why didn't I come back as a woman? Why am I black? How does a five-year-old play a violin in a concert orchestra? I don't have the answers. Maybe it's more about what we did learn and are here to learn than who we are. Perhaps I needed something visible that would affect how people react to me instead of a hidden wound that no one could see. Maybe I just wasn't educated enough to make a better choice. Or maybe it's purely a matter of chance, like winning the lottery. I don't know. All I know is, regression helped me and that's what is important. I accept it and what it has done for me, even if I can't explain it. If it helps, I incorporate it into my life.

"As far as Honey really being the woman you killed, I don't know. But doesn't it make you stop and think why she is a part of your life now? Who or what coincidence worked that out? Yes, George, I think she is more than a symbol. I don't think it is an accident. Weiss talks about soulmates, and Jung about synchronicity. Maybe you and Honey resolved the conflict and unified the families by marrying and are destined to meet in many lifetimes to help each other learn and grow."

"Guys, I feel like Ebba's lord—the one giving the orders for reasons that only I know, and yet I expect people to act out of faith in me. Fear is not what I want decisions to be based upon. I realize we don't have to eliminate the relationship or one member of it to change things.

Carmine's intensity entranced them. "I see Juaquin choosing to hate the world and everyone in it and seeking revenge. What if he had sworn to return and make the world a safer and more loving place? When I heard his final words, I knew why I chose this life. No one will do to my family what was done to that boy's family. I thought that would bring me peace. Instead, it has led to more fear, unhappiness, and pain. I am doing to other children's families what was done to me. I am no better than the people who killed my family.

"Someone sometime must stand up and choose to love their children more than they hate their enemies. Today I am making that choice. I will honor that boy, and my grandson, by choosing life and love. I will give what I want.

"People say I'm not like other so-called goodfellas because I don't say 'fuck you' all the time and don't want to cut every troublemaker's balls off. Some of that was due to my grandfather always telling me to watch what I said, but I think another part is due to that boy. There is a part of me that has always despised violence.

"Up until today, I have talked the talk but not walked the walk. What else has changed me? My grandson. My life suddenly makes sense because of what has happened to him. I was devastated. My world was turned upside down.

"I told him, 'Junior, I'm going to make that son of a bitch pay for what he did to you. He won't be hurting anyone else when I'm done with him.'"

"And Junior said, 'Poppie, you're being just like him. Will getting even help? Will more pain help? Will killing help? Will it make me better? Time will take care of him. He needs our help—and our love. too.'

"The kid brought me to tears. Now I can see the choice I need to make. I will talk to my associates and it doesn't matter anymore what their reaction will be. I can't let my grandson down."

George was moved to tears. "Carmine, I realize what a mess I've made out of my life trying to make up for the pain I caused. I tried so hard and ended up resenting and blaming Honey for my problems and guilt."

"My life as a therapist will be very different because of what the three of us have shared," said Jon. "I now realize how much we can learn from one another. The therapist can receive therapy too. The hard part is taking the time to stop and listen for the answers to the big questions"

Carmine clapped his hands. "Amen! Jon, get your CD player out. All we need now is a little gospel music."

CHAPTER 22

While Jon had been working with the men Inge completed her therapy work with the women. After her last session with the women, Inge sought out Jon.

"When I come down for the fall picnic," she said, "I'd love to lead you all in a shared healing ritual."

"Great idea. I hope the entire day is a healing ritual. Also, would you mind putting together a few words for my final report? I see no indication that George represents a risk to anyone, and he certainly is not insane, incompetent, violent, or brain damaged as a result of his injuries."

"No problem. What happens if it rains?"

"It never does. Jung would have something nice to say about that. Some of the patients will be speaking. It should prove interesting, as always. Every patient who isn't violent, suicidal, or an escape risk is invited to attend with their significant others. Former patients are also invited back and encouraged to bring food, pets, and athletic equipment. It helps the staff to see people they have treated surviving in the real world."

———✳———

On the day of the picnic Inge came early, went to the group therapy room, and placed the chairs in a circle. She laughed, thinking about George discussing his birthday present.

"For my birthday," he said, "Honey gave me this bracelet inscribed with WWLD. No, it's not Lassie. She wants me to lighten up. It's stands for What Would Lucy Do?"

Carmine had shared his new role model was Don Quixote de La Mancha. They were both Dons, but he preferred Don Quixote to Don Carmine. He started calling Maria Dulcey after watching *Man of La Mancha* on cable and witnessing Don Q transform the barmaid Aldonza into the beautiful Dulcinea with his tenderness. He bought the soundtrack of the musical on CD and rehearsed in the limo. Michael and Gabriel learned to close the partition.

Carmine even went so far as to put on his sneakers and jog after Maria one day.

"To what do I owe this surprise?" Maria had asked.

"I just wanted to enjoy the pleasure of your company," replied Carmine, panting. "And like you keep saying: I need the exercise."

"Carmine, you are so sweet to do this."

"Dulcey, I shall run after you for as long as I live."

Inge's reveries were interrupted by Jon and Judy arriving in the therapy room. The others followed shortly thereafter and took their seats in the chair circle.

"Please sit facing your spouse and share what your soul wants you to say," said Inge. "This is a sacred moment to share what is within you that may never have been said before."

Hokmah volunteered to start. He looked into Judy's eyes and said, "I have a deep love for you and apologize for any pain I may have caused you in the past or will in the future. I thank you for your love during this trying time of transition in our lives and hope you'll continue to forgive and love me as I learn and devote myself to being kind and loving. I am forever grateful to you for your love and friendship. I promise to remain open to your criticism and to take singing lessons. I understand now that marriage is not about two people but about their relationship and I hope to provide you with the husband you deserve."

"So, you are going to find me another husband," said Judy, with tongue in cheek. "How nice of you! Lighten up and find a role model that has a sense of humor so we can hold our love together with laughter. We need to share the joy, not just the pain. Perhaps the children can teach us about living in the moment. I will continue putting my love and my notes into your things and our life to help us live and love each day. And when you come home, please don't bring your office with you. What makes you a good psychiatrist doesn't provide your family with the dad and husband we need."

George and Honey followed. They opened their hearts, agreeing to spend more time together, away from the world and all their responsibilities. They laughed about the number of pets they were each allowed to have.

George said, "I no longer need to name the pets. I'll leave that to the children."

Honey said, "I promise to remove the litter box from your office, quit smoking, and turn the lights off. And out of my love for you, George, I shall always treat you like a dog."

"And I shall treat you like a kitten."

Love provided the freedom to laugh and cry together.

Inge interjected: "Will George Burns and Gracie Allen please finish their list of significant changes later?"

Childlike humor was the mortar that held what love constructed together.

Carmine spoke quietly about his new life and where it might lead him.

"I am fearful, but I'm not sure what I'm afraid of: fear of change or separation. Fear is new to me. I must understand it and learn from it that fear is to protect us from threats to our life. Otherwise, its effect becomes self-destructive. What I have learned is that words can become swords, and with swords you can kill or cure. The choice is ours. Though it's hard for me to buy that old Robert Browning line, 'Grow old along with me, the best is yet to be.'"

"Carmine, I love you and married you because of what I saw in you the day we met," said Maria. "We shall overcome your fears of the future together. And we can grow young by enjoying the present. Fear may protect you from danger but imagined fears do the opposite."

Inge said, "Would everyone please rise and embrace your loved one."

The Hokmahs and Dingfelders stepped forward. They cried, laughed, embraced, and became one.

Maria moved towards Carmine, who remained transfixed. She reached for his hand as a frightened child's words poured from his mouth, and tears burst forth.

"Fear grips my heart. I don't want to risk suffering the way I did when I lost everyone, I loved in my past life. How can I love when I don't know how to deal with all the things, I don't have power over, and never will? The closer people get, the more I will be hurt. The more I love, the more loved ones I will lose. I don't know. I don't know. It's so hard to live with loss. There is no solution to my fears."

Maria embraced him. "Carmine, do you remember our first meeting at the Hyatt in Hilton Head? Philip Myers was at the piano singing love songs. I stood up to go to the powder room and bumped into you. You had to grab me to keep me from falling. It was very special.

"We looked into each other's eyes and walked down the hall together. When I came out of the powder room you were waiting for me. I felt flattered and excited. We walked back to the lounge. I took your hand and asked if you'd like to dance. And you acted like an embarrassed teenager. I had no idea who you were. It just seemed like it was meant to be.

"Phil sang 'Someone to Watch Over Me.' I saw tears in your eyes. I could sense your discomfort. You said you had to go. You are not that lonely, frightened child anymore. I will watch over you. You will never be alone again. Carmine remember the only thing of permanence is love. There are no coincidences. When you identify and confront your fears magic happens."

She caressed his face and started to croon "'There's a somebody I'm longing to see...I hope that she...turns out to be...someone to watch over me.'"

As she sang, Carmine closed his eyes and held Maria as he had never held anyone before— knowing, for the first time, that you can't be separated from someone you love; and that love is the only thing which is immortal. The silence spoke for him.

Hokmah rose from his seat, "Let's finish with a group hug. Inge, please get in the middle, so we can thank you."

After the embrace they stepped out into the crisp autumn air, in stark contrast to the warmth of the room.

CHAPTER 23

The event was organized mayhem. A wonderful, chaotic day, like a college reunion. You couldn't tell patients from staff members. Name tags were the only means of identification.

Hokmah found Seltzer, Graham, and Dunklee's families sitting at a table together. He was happy to have them experience the event and hoped it would affect how they treated those they had to deal with in their work. The men stepped away from the table. He thanked them for their patience, handed Dunklee his report, briefly discussed its contents and added a complimentary off-the-record word about Carmine. The day was like nothing he had ever experienced as a psychiatrist. Hokmah felt like he was spending the day with his entire family, including the troublemakers and the black sheep; they were all loved ones.

As he walked away, he saw Carmine join their group. He directed his comments to the two lawmen.

"I'm a changed man. Whatever you may have thought of me, or still do for that matter, is water under the bridge as far as I'm concerned. I'm a grandfather now, not a godfather; my past is not who I am.

"I'm giving you this envelope and permission to call me Poppie. The letter inside contains information related to the Benjamin case and a personal note.

I feel free to offer it to you because none of my associates were involved. Aside from this unsigned note, I will forever remain silent about the past."

Seltzer and Graham tore open the envelope, glanced briefly at the letter, looked knowingly at each other, and then read the note from Carmine aloud.

Dear Bubbles and Cookie,

In the future, if you have any judicial or relationship problems, feel free to contact me. I still have therapeutic family connections and may be able to help you eliminate your problems. If you ever hear that I am taking someone out, don't worry, they are referring to a dinner engagement.

Peace,

Poppie

When they finished reading and looked up, Carmine nodded and winked before taking his leave.

As Carmine walked across the grounds of Peaceful Acres he recalled the day, several weeks prior, he spoke to his associates, whom he felt deserved to hear about his decision from his own lips: that he had the courage to lose one life and find another. He hoped his father would be proud of him and his grandfather would understand.

"I asked you all here today to share a personal decision," Carmine had addressed the goombahs. "When I'm done speaking, I'll answer all your questions. Most of you are aware of the changes brought about by my dealings with Dingfelder. Because of my association with him and his psychiatrist, I have discovered things about myself and my past. With this new understanding, I feel it is time to change my life."

He was interrupted by the group's raucous protests. They sensed what he was about to say and were unwilling to accept his decision.

"Please, gentlemen, let me finish! I told you I would answer all your questions. This isn't about them. It's about me. Carmine Junior has taught me some lessons too. I can't be effective anymore with what I've learned. I would not be the kind of person you would be safe working with. My feelings would interfere. You want a godfather, not a grandfather making decisions.

"My new life will in no way endanger any of you. I will never dishonor our code of silence. You have my word. I hope we will still be family.

"The past is over. I don't feel guilty about it or blame anyone. I respect and honor my grandfather, but my life has to go in another direction now. This is not about judging anyone but about finding a new path.

"Hokmah and Dingfelder are no threat. You can trust them; I guarantee that, or I never would have continued to meet with them. I think their past behavior with the authorities verifies that. I will never reveal any information that may cause anyone in this room any problems. I have let the authorities know that, and that the Benjamin case had nothing to do with any of you. That is the last thing I will have to say to them about anything, and it should make your lives a little easier.

"I respect you and your concerns. I can only repeat I am a changed man. I shall remain your friend but not your business associate. We are still family, but I want to be a member of a larger family now. I hope you can live with that and let me live my life. If not, I'm ready for whatever the future brings. I have asked Mario to take over for me. He and I have always been close, and he is well aware of what it takes to run the show. Any questions?"

To a smattering of polite applause, Mario walked up and embraced him.

"What can I say? We are family and go back a long way together. Nothing can ever change that. I love you, you son of a bitch."

One by one, those present rose to embrace Carmine and wish him and his family well.

Carmine's reverie was interrupted by his granddaughter Maria tugging on his pants. "Grampa, I'm hungry."

"Me too, doll-face. Let's go get some grub at the buffet. I could eat a horse!"

Little Maria rolled her eyes. "Oh, Poppie, you could not!"

CHAPTER 24

After the buffet lunch, Hokmah went up on stage, turned on the microphone and faced his audience of resident patients, their family members, visitors and his special group connected to the three musketeers, George, Carmine and their connections, all seated or sitting on blankets across the large open lawn.

"Welcome to our fall picnic. We have many wise and talented people here today who will be sharing their wisdom and talent with us this afternoon.

"But first, I want to thank all of you for helping me become a better therapist and human being. I have learned that our patients, family, and co-workers are our greatest teachers. So please keep after me. I am always willing to learn. Your criticism polishes my mirror. I apologize for any pain I may have caused you and hope you can forgive me.

"Second, I saw the beneficial effect of amnesia on George Dingfelder's life. As a psychotherapist, I thought it would be very therapeutic if I could prescribe an amnesia pill, but you helped me to discover something better. Let me read you a description of it. If it were a new drug, every doctor would prescribe it.

"It is patient, kind, and envies no one. It is never boastful, nor conceited, nor rude; never selfish, nor quick to take offense. It keeps no score of wrongs; does not gloat over other's sins but delights in the truth. There is nothing it cannot face; there is no limit to its faith, its hope, and its endurance. It will never come to an end.

"In a word, there are three things that last forever: faith, hope, and love; but the greatest of them all is love. Love, my friends, is far better than amnesia. I have learned this from all of you.

"When you leave here today don't forget to love yourselves, your families, your neighbors, your friends, and most of all your enemies.

"I have learned that love is blind to our faults and weaknesses. So, as a physician, I want to start an epidemic of love blindness. You are all to be carriers of the disease and see to it that we inoculate everyone with the love bug. Reparent them by becoming their loving chosen parent.

"Last but not least, I want to thank all our partners and spouses for their love and kindness. And to remind you to let this season be a symbol in your life. Before you let go of the tree of life, reveal your beauty and uniqueness to the world like the fall leaves, and remember we are all the same color inside. Now it's time for you to share your words of wisdom. George, the stage is yours."

"Hi, I'm George Dingfelder, a surgeon. I am not telling you that because I want you as patients but because, like Hokmah, I have learned there is only one whole life policy: love. With it, we can all be life assurance agents and, as a surgeon, perform a faith lift.

"On a personal level, what has helped me most has been to view life as a puzzle. I now see difficulties as questions or problems to be solved. In this way my life has taken on new meaning; solutions appear I never would have been aware of before.

"I accept the reality that life is not unfair, but it certainly is difficult—something we all complain about. However, instead of whining I now learn from my difficulties and let them lead me to nourish myself in new ways. Like labor pains or an unfinished work of art.

"I want to thank Jon, Carmine, and Inge for helping us heal our relationships. And to our wives, God bless. May you all understand why, imitate how, and know when."

Hokmah recalled his first impression of George: like a frightened squirrel. He was a squirrel no longer. To thunderous applause, George fairly strutted off the stage into Honey's arms.

Carmine was up next.

"Good afternoon, ladies and gents. I'm Carmine Birsamatto. I want to thank my wife, my family, and my friends for helping me to become a new man. We are a team with much to do.

"I didn't come to deliver a sermon but to sing to my wife, Maria. Bear with me and don't leave because of my singing. Maria, thank you for always saying yes."

Carmine became Don Quixote for everyone to enjoy as he sang "Dulcinea" from *Man of La Mancha* in a baritone voice whose sincerity outweighed its wobbliness.

Tears, cheers, and applause filled the air. Maria came up and Carmine bent her over backwards with a kiss. His grandchildren teased him for months about his singing and kissing skills. Cries for an encore were heard. Carmine bowed and walked off the stage with Maria.

Hokmah turned to Willie the Mouseketeer, who earlier had requested to speak. "Willie, when the audience quiets down the stage is yours."

Before Willie could begin Jeff, a profoundly depressed resident Hokmah had confined to his room with an attendant, came forward and took the microphone. Hokmah was very concerned until Jeff's attendant reassured him.

Jeff began in a monotone. "I have been here several weeks, depressed and suicidal. I felt that life sucked and most people sucked. My feeling was, if you woke up one day and the world was beautiful, and everyone loved one another and you were no longer suffering, you must be dead. Frankly, I didn't care whether I lived or died until today. Today I realize there is another option; you can be at a Peaceful Acres picnic. You have taught me that I can choose my attitude and live one day at a time. So, if any of you are considering suicide tomorrow, think about what you are going to do tonight. It might make you change your mind."

There was polite, somewhat uncomfortable applause. Jeff turned with a faint trace of a smile and handed the microphone to Willie.

"Like Jeff, I am well today for many reasons. First, for those who are unaware, is the fact that Peaceful Acres is run by a Mouseketeer. This fact gave me confidence in my therapy.

"I want to award this cap to the Chief Mouseketeer." He presented Hokmah with an authentic Mouseketeer cap and asked him to remain on stage.

"Because of the work Dr. Hokmah has done, the staff will not be known as the Mouseketeers, even if it is my personal preference, but by a much more appropriate name. By unanimous agreement of the patients, I hereby declare, from this day forth you will be known as The Dream Team."

Willie handed the staff T-shirts with THE DREAM TEAM printed on the front. They hugged Willie and sat down wearing their new employee shirts.

"And now I want you to meet my wife. When I came here as Mickey Mouse everyone assumed, I was nuts and, therefore, married to Minnie Mouse. When Jon took over my therapy, he asked me why I didn't call her by her given name. He knew from my records her name was Beth. Now I shall reveal the reason. Minnie, please."

A woman, no taller than four feet six inches, came forward.

"Her nickname has always been Minnie, on account of her short stature. Now that you all know that Dr. Hokmah can discharge me as cured." Willie laughed.

Newman walked over to Hokmah. "I didn't realize how personal these events were, Jon. I have been quite moved; now I know why the sun shines on your picnic. It just goes to show you what can come from a good knock on the head."

While they were talking, Honey took over the microphone.

"Please remember, we are all capable of change. We all have the potential. When desire and intention—not just wishful thinking—are present, lives are altered. When you decide to be a loving person you change yourself, and the people around you will change as a byproduct of your love. So, rehearse and practice until you get it right. Success is I can. Failure is I can't."

"Bless you and thank you, Honey." Jon and Honey embraced.

Hokmah returned to the stage to introduce the choir and join them, singing softly off-key, in the back row.

After several songs by the choral group their leader announced, "In closing, we shall sing 'Amazing Grace' and then 'He.' Join us if you know the words."

Hokmah listened for Danny and himself.

EPILOGUE

D unklee handed down his favorable ruling based upon Hokmah's report and Carmine's off-the-record contribution.

Carmine received a box in the mail with no return address. He was a bit reluctant to open it. Maria did, while he was out, and found a baseball cap with the letters FBI printed on the front panel. The accompanying note said it stood for Full Blooded Italian. He had some interesting responses when he wore it in public.

In the years that followed the three remained close friends, vacationing together, attending the annual picnic, and sharing a reverence for life. George altered his surgical practice and took sessions for training as a psychotherapist. He ran a smaller, more intimate practice with less concern for the dollar. He also started a therapy group for patients with life-threatening illnesses and other mind-body issues. His practice increased due to his reputation in the community.

George and Carmine started Exceptional Properties, a real estate company which restored old houses and converted them into shelters for abused women and homeless pets. Often, the women and pets adopted each other and a new life. The dogs were good role models and very effective therapy for the control of abusive spouses.

George brought pet therapy to Peaceful Acres. The grounds were filled with geese, ducks, goats, rabbits, and pets of all kinds. The animals were intuitive and assisted the staff. A black Lab named Doc would sit next to a patient or sleep in his room until the staff became aware of the patient's previously undetected needs. Two crazy toy poodles were named Pro and Zac because they lifted everyone's spirits. The holistic patients dubbed them St. John and Wort.

The craziest pets on the premises were a hallucinating cat and her three kittens. They were always chasing their tails and imaginary mice and getting high on catnip. They helped the therapists working with psychotic patients and drug addicts. The mother cat was named Psycho and her kittens Halloo, Sin, and Nation.

Honey quit smoking and moved the litter boxes out of George's office into the playroom where she and the kids could take care of them. The following year she gave birth to a son she and George named Jonathan Carmine Dingfelder, or JC for short. George took over the care of the litter boxes during her pregnancy so she wouldn't be exposed to any disease-causing organisms. Honey was impressed how one could abandon the past when love and intimacy were present. She and George learned that wisdom derived from love and intelligence is far better than amnesia.

Carmine became an active fundraiser for any cause helping children, animals, or HIV-positive teenagers. He learned from an HIV+ young man that the disease wasn't evil but failing to respond with compassion to the person with the disease was. He used his past effectively. People found it hard to refuse his requests due to his Family connections. He took up jogging and started doing low mileage runs with large donations per mile from his sponsors. His former associates loved coming out to heckle him as he trotted along wearing his FBI cap.

Carmine became president of Saint Luke's Hospital's and Peaceful Acres' auxiliaries. Few had the courage to run against him; he made the volunteer staff offers they couldn't refuse, especially with Michael and Gabriel around. There was still an element of Don Carmine in his relationships. His family and coworkers frequently pointed that out to him, and with time he became more the grandfather and less the godfather.

He and Maria opened their lives and their home to foster children. They exercised together and were the talk of the neighborhood. When the Birsamatto herd come rumbling down the street on their morning jog or bike ride, all the local traffic stopped.

Carmine bought the Cape Cod house that had formerly been their summer rental, and his family spent their vacations getting to know each other again. They loved the bike trails and jogging on the beach. Carmine Jr. thrilled everyone by how well he responded to his HIV antiretroviral treatment and the family's love and support. He was their teacher, keeping them living in the moment. He and Carmine often spoke at schools about unsafe sex and drugs.

The following year's meeting of the American Psychiatric Association was scheduled at the Menninger Foundation in Topeka, Kansas. The APA invited Hokmah to present a workshop about his practice and personal transformation. He flew out for the start of the meeting and ran into Inge in the hotel lobby.

"I'm getting married this summer and my future hubby is not a doctor," she told him. "You'll all be getting invitations to the wedding."

When Hokmah opened his luggage, he found a note that said, "I Love You, Dumpling. The children love you and the cats and dogs love you. Call us often. XOXOX " Below that was his wife's sketch of the kids and pets. He laughed as he unpacked and found grapes and bananas wrapped in bubble wrap. He was touched by how simple it was to say, "I love you."

He met Dr. Karl Menninger, who was still a dynamic individual at ninety-six. Hokmah really enjoyed talking to him about his life's work, reading his books, and seeing his office collection of books and memorabilia. Here was a man whose footsteps had made a path others could follow. Hokmah mentioned he had an uncle who was ninety-four.

Menninger heaved a wistful sigh. "I wish I were ninety-four again."

The next morning before Hokmah dressed for his run; he took out his razor and shaved his face. He felt like a newborn. Body and spirit were out there uncovered for everyone to see. He knew he would be teased about it, but it didn't matter. He went out and started his run, enjoying the change.

After jogging a few miles, he spotted a small church cemetery and thought of George. He ran over to read the words of wisdom. As he jogged along the gravel path, he noticed a headstone with the names Salvatore and Rosa Petonito. Salvatore's Army service record was carved into the stone and a small American flag flew over the grave. On the lower portion of their stone was a small area with the name Furphy carved in capital letters, and beneath it, in smaller letters, Sex. On the stone was an enamel photo of the couple and their little three-legged dog.

His feelings overwhelmed him. Then he saw a badly chipped stone within an area enclosed by a low metal railing and the names Gilbert, Martha, and Daniel Hoffman. Beneath their birth and death dates were their respective epitaphs:

"His Life Taught Us How To Live And His Death How To Die."

"Wife And Mother To All."

"Together Forever. Thanks For Your Love—I Can Take It With Me.

Jon burst into tears and knelt, feeling faint. He realized for the first time why the song "Danny Boy," as sung by Celtic Women, had such an emotional impact upon him, and why he was always telling Alexa to play it over and over when he was home.

After a few minutes he rose and raced back to the Menninger Foundation where he drove everyone to distraction until they located Dr. Karl Menninger.

"Dr. Menninger, it's very important to me, for personal reasons, to know if you remember a social worker named Martha Hoffman? And treating her teenage son, Danny? I know it's a little crazy to ask about someone you might have known six or more decades ago, but this is really very important to me."

"That's quite a long time ago and I see a lot of people. What was his problem?"

"Danny was depressed following the accidental death of his father and the suicide of his teacher, a Mr. Roget."

"I don't recall them. I'll ask my secretary to pull the records and get right on it."

"Bless you. Here's my room number. Have them call as soon as they learn anything."

Jon couldn't get the cemetery out of his mind. Was it true? My God if it were true should he report it at the workshop later today? Would he be called delusional?

The phone rang as he was dressing. It was Dr. Menninger's secretary, who said she had some information.

"Martha Hoffman was a staff member in the late forties and early fifties. There's a chart for a Daniel Hoffman but Dr. Karl never saw him. There's a note in his record stating he committed suicide the day before his appointment. I'm sorry, Dr. Hokmah, but that's the only information we could find."

"Thank you."

The phone dropped from his hand. With tears running down his cheeks he drove to the cemetery, where he knelt at Danny's grave and told the youth how much he had taught him about love and forgiveness and the people they had helped.

Whether it made any sense or not, he needed to do it for completion. Who was listening? What would he tell George and Carmine when he got home? Should he take photographs of the headstones? He kept pouring out his life story to Danny until he felt a hand upon his shoulder. He was afraid to turn and see who it was until he heard a voice.

"Are you alright? I'm the minister here, Reverend David Young. Were you related to the Hoffmans? Would you like to come inside? We can sit and talk. You can come in and rest in the sanctuary if you don't want to talk."

"I'm fine, Reverend. It's just been a very emotional day for me. Yes, the Hoffmans and I are related, in a manner of speaking. It's a long story. Actually, I'm grateful to the Hoffmans for many things."

Reverend Young didn't press Hokmah for details. Rather, he rhapsodized on the gorgeous day. "October is God's favorite month. With the leaves changing color and the beautiful sunsets, one just can't help feeling the touch of our Creator.

"I can't help but feel the leaves are a message to uncover our beauty before we let go of the tree of life just the way the sun sets in glorious color.

"I think God loves us just the way we are, even when we do shake the family tree a little. There I go, sermonizing to one person on his knees. Once a minister, always a minister. I'll let you get on with whatever you need to do. If you're sure you don't need anything, I'll be going inside now. Though, to tell you the truth, I feel closer to God out here. Bless you, my son, and peace be with you."

Hokmah finished his goodbyes to the Hoffmans.

That afternoon he took some good-natured teasing about his clean-shaven appearance; smooth as a baby's behind was the comparison he heard most often. Later in the day, while he shared his experience and spoke from his heart, the sound of silence made it difficult for him to think or speak.

When he finished, everyone remained silent and immobile. As he gathered his papers and turned to leave, one member of the audience rose and began to applaud. The sound broke the spell and was followed by a crescendo of applause. Hokmah was stunned by the response. He returned to the podium in tears.

"I want to thank you for the opportunity you have given me to speak today. Your response and acceptance mean a great deal to me."

His personal risk and vulnerability all seemed worthwhile now.

"Any questions from the audience? Yes, Bruce, good to see you back again at our reunion."

"Jon, one cannot question a sermon. However, that doesn't mean we haven't benefited greatly from it. God bless you for having the courage to live the experience and share it with us. We have all learned a great deal today. It is said there is only one thing more truthful than the truth: a story. Thank you for sharing your story and may we all have the courage to live our stories as you have lived yours."

"Bruce, I'm going to take advantage of your response and my feeling of safety to leave you with this final message. My friends, please remember that life is a series of beginnings. How can I say this when we all experience change and loss? Because life goes on, and with it the opportunity to begin the never-ending beginning. We all know time passes, books are read, the show ends, people expire, and the sun sets; but then the next day begins. We now live a different life revealing the effects of time, knowledge, death, and life upon us.

"What I have to say has all been said before. Information is useless without revelation which leads to inspiration and transformation. I hope you will fill your lifetime and therapy with inspiration and not expiration and get to know yourself by your actions. Remember a graduation is called a commencement and not a termination. Life has no endings, only beginnings."

Hokmah walked off the stage to begin his life. Their applause followed and he took it with him.

ABOUT THE AUTHOR

Dr. Siegel, who prefers to be called Bernie, not Dr. Siegel, was born in Brooklyn, NY. He attended Colgate University and Cornell University Medical College. He holds membership in two scholastic honor societies, Phi Beta Kappa and Alpha Omega Alpha and graduated with honors. His surgical training took place at Yale New Haven Hospital, West Haven Veteran's Hospital and the Children's Hospital of Pittsburgh. He retired from practice as an assistant clinical professor of surgery at Yale of general and pediatric surgery in 1989 to speak to patients and their caregivers.

In 1986 his first book, *Love. Medicine & Miracles* was published. This event redirected his life. In 1989 *Peace, Love & Healing* and in 1993 *How To Live Between Office Visits* followed. Bernie's realization that we all need help dealing with the difficulties of life, not just the physical ones, led to Bernie writing his fourth book in 1998 *Prescriptions for Living*. It helps people to become aware of the eternal truths and wisdom of the sages through Bernie's stories and insights rather than wait a personal disaster. Since then he has written many enlightening books including his most recent When You Realize How Perfect Everything Is with his grandson Charlie Siegel.

Learn more at www.BernieSiegelMD.com